A FEW SMALL STONES

A Collection of Stories by

Marilyn Ogus Katz

Published by Unsolicited Press

www.unsolicitedpress.com

Copyright © 2018 Marilyn Ogus Katz

All Rights Reserved.

Editor: Rubie Grayson

Editorial Assistant: Adam Kelly

Some stories were previously published:

"A Few Small Stones" *Hadassah Magazine*, August/September, 2016

"Uncle Sol Comes To America" *Tupolo Quarterly* semi-finalist Winter Prose Contest, 2016

"Life List" *Writer's Digest Best Short Shorts 2015*

"Ta Da!" *Jewish Currents*, Summer, 2016

"Witness To History" *Persimmon Tree*, Fall 2016

For information, contact the publisher at

info@unsolicitedpress.com

Unsolicited Press Books are distributed to the trade by Ingram.

Printed in the United States of America.

ISBN: 978-1-947021-15-0

Dedication

These stories explore what it means to grow up in an
extended immigrant family. I thank my immediate family:
my companion George Petty, my son and daughter-in-law,
Jimmy and Dena Katz, my daughter and son-in-law Emily
and Eduardo Anhalt, and my granddaughters Erica and
Ariela Anhalt. George, Emily, Erica, and Ariela are
writers and editors themselves, read drafts, raising issues for
possible revision.

Four other families encouraged me in my life and
work, my mother Rebecca Simon Ogus, grandmother
Sarah Simon, close cousins Muriel Schwartz and Michael
Staub, father Samuel Ogus, and cousins especially Herta
Levine, Garry Goldberg, Max and Olga Dolgicer, my
husband, the late Maurice "Mac" Katz, his sister, Mildred
Strauss, nieces and nephews particularly Madeline, Jay and
Peter, but also Eliza, Brian and Carolyn Strauss, Erin
Brigham, and the attentive Marjorie Lynn and her sister

Lisa Blumenthal and finally George's family, the Leouses, Adairs and Pettys.

Friends became readers, and a few made comments: Three of the dearest, Libby Moroff, Ruth Rosen, and Beatrice Frank, did not live to see this collection published. Bea read everything with enthusiasm. I treasure Libby's interest and her wise and careful readings. Her question about "Secrets and Lies" strengthened that story. An articulate critic, Ruth supplied details of the era. I am indebted to her for "The Garden Cafeteria," named after her father's Lower East Side restaurant, now a legend.

The fine author and dear friend Francine Klagsbrun, had faith in the title story and in me, but also Janet Segal, Barbara Fields, Phyllis Schwartz, Catherine Nicholas, Dick Shoup, Lila and Walter Croen, Saul Moroff, JoAnne Wasserman, Stuart Marques, Karen Greenspan, Phyllis Vine, Barbara Cohn, Helen and Lou Lowenstein, Judy Freed and Gerry Weiss, Nancy and Joe Amiel, Mari Gold, Alice Kramer, Jane Orans, Marshall Taylor, Kathy Neustadt, Nancy Barcelo, and Janet Kleinman. Sarah

Lawrence colleagues: Presidents Alice Stone Ilchman, Michele Tolela Meyers (also a fiction writer) Joan Harrison, Daphne Dumas, Beverly Fox, Libby Kane, Deans Ilya Wachs and Barbara Kaplan, Priscilla Hawkins, Prema Samuel, Celia Regan, Beverly Fox, Bob Cameron. Faculty: particularly Charlotte Doyle, Margery Franklin, Bella Brodski, Ann and Joe Lauinger, Fred Smoler.

Thank you, Dr. David Lindy and Dr. Lisa Mandl. Early mentors: poet/professor/friend Diana Ben Merre, author/activist/ artist/friend Bel Chevigny, and the author Abigail Thomas, leader of our Tuesday Night Babes. Today I am inspired by Laurence Bush, the intrepid editor of *c* and Ed McCann of read650.

I feel fortunate to have an agent/ friend, Laurie Liss of Sterling, Lord Literistic, who always knows exactly what's wrong with a work and demands revision after revision.

Finally I thank my responsive editor at Unsolicited Press, Rubie Grayson, and the vigilant editorial assistant

Adam Kelly, whose concern made A FEW SMALL STONES stronger and more coherent work.

FOR MY FAMILY

Mac and George

Jimmy and Dena

Emily and Eduardo

Erica and Ariela

Contents

PART ONE

A FEW SMALL STONES

My cousin Harvey only calls when there's a death in the family. He's the custodian of our cemetery plot and the first to know. Harvey will tell the cemetery workers to 'open the grave,' as though beneath the deceptive lid of grass, an empty space is waiting.

This time it's our cousin Florence who died of a heart attack at eighty-four. I don't drive, so once again, Harvey suggests we go to the cemetery together. We haven't seen each other since the last funeral. But over sixty years ago, I babysat him as he toddled around the coffee table, blond ringlets bouncing around his neck. Each mile on the Long Island Expressway takes us back to the past we share.

Harvey and I grew up at that cemetery. Some families take pride in a homestead, a farm, or a compound on a river, but ours struggled to preserve a patch of burial ground. In the 1930s, our grandmother and her five younger siblings, recent immigrants from Poland, started the Feldman Family Organization and bought a cemetery plot on Long Island with sixty graves. They insisted we

Jews own a piece of land from which no one could ever turn us away.

The family met on the second Saturday of each month in a member's home. We were so many and of various generations that even as a child I knew the difference between an uncle and a great uncle, or a second cousin and a first cousin once removed. My grandmother held forth in the living rooms, her gold watch swinging on a long chain like a pendulum below her waist. Bubbe, a leader at the Bialystoker Home for the Aged and The Workmen's Circle, kept to an agenda even in a room of her boisterous brothers and sisters. Maintaining the cemetery plot might be the first item of business, but the family organization also sent money to an eldest sister in Poland, raised funds for the poor, planned the Hanukkah party, decided where to hold the annual picnic and who would bring what dish. Bubbe embraced the democracy of her adopted country and encouraged debate, but she always got her way.

We children chased one another and hid in unfamiliar rooms and closets. Most of us fell asleep, snuggling among the abandoned coats on the bed, awakening red and overheated and staggering out into the cold night air with imprints of coat buttons on our cheeks. By the time I was ten or twelve, my great uncles and great aunts began to die, and I visited our plot again and again, as easy around the gravestones as on the swings at the state park where we went for our picnic every June.

When Harvey pulls up in the car, I hand him a hard candy.

"Tradition," I explain.

"You know, Alice," he says. "*My* mother used to bring hard candies, too." My mother and Harvey's were sisters.

"It's going to be a long day." He clutches the wheel and peers into the rain. I'm glad I brought my umbrella.

"I wonder what they'll do when I'm not around anymore," Harvey says. Most people in our family die of heart disease and he has already had heart surgery.

"Maybe your son could take over," I suggest.

"I think Scott's gone to the cemetery once, for his mom's funeral. He lives in Santa Barbara. Been there a couple of years."

"Really? I didn't know. How long is it since Cynthia died?"

"Eleven years this January." Harvey says, his voice tight. "I feel as though I've been robbed."

"I know what you mean," I say. "Bob's been gone almost twenty." But it's my husband who was robbed. I've lived to watch our grandchildren grow up. Cynthia and Bob are buried about fifteen feet from each other. In the Jewish tradition, Harvey and I will place small stones on their footstones today.

When my husband met the family, an uncle asked him for sixty dollars to buy two graves. Bob was twenty-eight. "Our first piece of real estate," he managed to crack as he peeled off the bills. I would wait until the last minute to tell Bob about a family event, and that made it worse. I also couldn't admit to my mother that he didn't want to go. I should have insisted we were an independent couple with plans of our own, but I was afraid of my mother and Bubbe. No matter how old I got, they could always make me feel like they had left me on the school steps to wait until dark. I was even willing to abandon my husband and go alone. Now, my Bob is spending eternity with relatives he didn't want to see one evening a month.

"Our family was so close when we were kids," I say. "Now, our children don't even know one another. You never told me Scott moved. What's with this strictly funeral relationship we have? Surely, we can do better."

"We used to have fun, didn't we?" Harvey says. "Like that New Year's when you let me stay up until midnight and we leaned out the window and banged pots and pans against the sill. You were the best babysitter, Alice. No one else came close."

But he doesn't apologize or promise to call me between deaths.

"And I loved the picnics, when the older cousins would let us younger boys run bases," Harvey continues. "Remember those baseball games?"

"Of course. I thought the guys were really cute." They stripped down to their thin white ribbed undershirts and, after two hours in the hot sun, they all smelled the same. Comforting, and strong, like some pungent spice. "And the mothers warmed the babies' milk bottles on the grill right next to the hotdogs and hamburgers," I remind Harvey.

"Hmm. Not exactly kosher."

"You know a committee planned the picnics for months. Then, one year it poured as hard as today, and at the next meeting, Uncle Herman announced, 'Next year when we have our picnic, let's have it on a nice day.'" I imitate his singsong.

Harvey laughs. "Did he really say that?"

We drive through the gates towards a miniature skyline of gray monuments, so unlike the green lawns of our childhood. We pass the turn-off to the cemetery building and parking lot. Generally, we stopped there to use the bathroom, register, and meet the hearse. I would follow my mother down the steep wooden stairs into the Ladies Room and into a narrow stall with translucent toilet paper. I washed at a gray washbasin and peered into a rippled tin mirror. The harsh fumes of cleaning fluid stung my eyes, and I wondered about the dizzy distance between being a child and dying.

Harvey wants to go directly to the family plot. We study the changed landmarks. A giant mound of landfill rises at the edge of the cemetery.

7

"They don't dump garbage there anymore," Harvey says, but I see seagulls circling. The landfill appeared around the time Bob died. As the rabbi spoke over his grave, a yellow dump truck wove up the hill, piling waste and refuse into what must be the only mountain in Suffolk County. It still upsets me, but Bob would have laughed.

"How could we have missed it," Harvey says, edging to the curb alongside the Feldman family plot. Without thinking, I say, "We'll do better next time."

"There used to be a lawn right here where we tailgated after unveilings," Harvey says. "Someone always brought a folding bridge table. There was schnapps for the grown-ups, with apple juice and honey cake for the kids."

"Another kind of picnic."

"We were kids. What did we know? Everyone who died seemed ancient."

People are gathering for the service, and Harvey and I step into the downpour. I clutch the spokes of my umbrella. I don't recognize any of the mourners, except Seymour, the husband of the cousin who died, his widowed sister, his grown son and daughter and Harvey's younger brother whom I hardly know. We are a small family above ground.

Florence's coffin sinks downward on its canvas stretcher. The rain strengthens the smell of newly turned loam. The rabbi is asking us to place a shovelful of earth on the casket. A few closer to the grave take their turns, slow and hesitant. The soil is wet and heavy, the shovel hard to lift and turn. I brace myself for the earthen thud and scatter of pebbles that assault the pine box again and again.

I walk along the pathway to my parents' graves and Bob's, pass Bubbe's and Zayde's, and stop to read the names of Bubbe's brothers and sisters. It's like the roll call she took at family meetings: "all present and accounted for." I see and hear each of them, talking and gesticulating, trampling on one another's sentences. Opposite lie some of their children and then, further along, Bubbe's three daughters and their husbands, including Harvey's parents and mine. I pluck a few small stones from the drenched soil and place them on my mother's and father's footstones. I turn towards Bob's and let a pure white pebble slip from my dirt-stained fingers. "I can't bear what I'm doing to you," he often said when he was dying. I want to tell him I'm all right, the children and the grandchildren too. I want us to laugh together again about the relatives who argued over which shrubs to plant on the graves as they reached for pieces of roast chicken and potato kugel. If my own grave weren't waiting under the grass next to Bob, I would probably choose cremation.

"Alice…Alice!" Harvey calls. He's at the curb near the car, talking to his brother. At my funeral, Harvey can introduce himself and his brother to my children.

"It's sad," I say on the drive back, "how the family fell apart. Your parents and mine refused to see each other for years. They only got together because Bubbe was dying. I watched you learn to walk. I used to quote the funny things you said. Our parents stayed mad and I was just a kid and I couldn't do anything about it."

Harvey presses buttons on the car radio. "That was a long time ago," he says, barely audible.

"You know my father took your dad into his business only as a favor to my mother. He trained him. And then your father went off with Dad's top salesman and his biggest customers and started a competing company. Our business suffered, and my mom blamed herself."

"You don't know the whole story, Alice." Harvey turns off the radio. "We couldn't forgive your dad. He owed mine $10,000 and never gave it back. My father couldn't pay for my Bar Mitzvah."

"And you believed him?" I can barely speak. "Does that sound like my father? He supported half the family. Every hard-luck story got a handout. "

"It doesn't, but…"

I won't say what I want to. Everyone knew Harvey's dad, my Uncle Phil, kept a mistress. That's probably why he had no money for the Bar Mitzvah. But to lie, to blame *my* dad, divide the sisters, and keep Harvey and me apart for so long? What's wrong with Harvey? How could he trust that man? My face is hot, but Harvey's jaw remains clenched. Stubborn. Yet after Harvey and I are gone, that's it. We're the only ones left who remember the explosive great aunt we called "Vesuvius", the other who knitted sweaters with armholes so tight we couldn't move, the great uncle who paid for my mother's piano lessons, the second cousin who made gefilte fish every Passover in a big metal grinder, or our Bubbe who marched through the city streets to demand the vote for women. Bubbe believed the

11

cemetery plot would draw us all together year after year, but soon our family's cherished piece of earth will fill with distant relatives who won't know or care about that once vibrant community of immigrants.

As we approach my corner, the rain lightens, and the sky clears. I slam the door and Harvey pulls away with my drenched old umbrella on the floor.

UNCLE SOL COMES TO AMERICA

Uncle Sol wears a hairnet to bed every night like an old lady. That's why his brown hair sticks to his head like it was painted on. He came on an ocean liner from Riga in Latvia where he grew up with Daddy, and he sleeps on a folding cot in the dinette under the calendar with the sunflower for August. Because Uncle Sol is in the dinette, we have to eat in the front hall. When anyone opens the door, you push your chair in.

I finish my chocolate pudding and take my dish into the kitchen, but Uncle Sol never helps clear the table. He's already sitting in Daddy's armchair next to the piano. He pokes his glasses up on his nose with his finger. "Why don't you join me for some after dinner conversation, Alice." Sometimes he talks to me like we're kings and queens.

I lean against the chair and Uncle Sol tells me I'm old enough to learn the family secrets. Like how Daddy got the scar on his lip. I know all about the scar. He stole Mr. Davidoff's horse and wagon and the horse kicked him.

Daddy always points to the little white caterpillar on his lip like he's bragging. It's not a family secret; it's just the opposite.

"He was all bloody, but our mama spanked him anyway," Uncle Sol is saying, "What can I tell you, Alice, your daddy got into a lot of trouble."

"What else?"

"Well he wasn't good like you. You know, back in Bausk—that's the village in Latvia where we lived when we were children—the boys had to go to "chedar" to study Hebrew. One time the rabbi fell asleep and your Daddy glued his long white beard to the desk. All the boys in the class shouted. The rabbi jerked his head up and cried out in pain."

"Ouch!" I say. "But I'm not good all the time."
Everyone knows stories don't come from being good.

"I told Mama no one can learn from someone who's always falling asleep," Uncle Sol says. "Every boy in the class was miserable, but only Abe did something about it. I was the one who had to make the excuses to Mama."

"Do you have more?"

"Well, your father saved my life. I wouldn't be sitting here if it wasn't for your daddy. He pulled me out after I fell through the ice. The water was freezing and he could have fallen in with me, but that didn't stop him. He was a hero."

"I don't know about that," Daddy says, "but I wasn't going to let you drown so Mama could give me that look and say, 'Why? Why did it have to be Sol?' She yelled at me anyway. She said I shouldn't take you skating."

"She wasn't an easy woman, our Mama," Uncle Sol says.

"She liked you better." Daddy's looking out the window. He's far away in his head where he is a lot of the time.

"That's not so. You were the man of action, not like Papa always with the books. She wanted you to take over the store. You didn't have to leave Riga, Abe. If you didn't like retail and the long hours, you could have gone into manufacturing like me. Did you know Alice, your father came to this country when he was only seventeen? He didn't know a word of English. Not like your Uncle Sol. Mama pinned a piece of paper to his jacket that said,

15

'Negaunee, Mich." He didn't even know "Mich" was the name of a state in America. Where Mama's relatives lived. Michigan."

Even I know Michigan and I'm only going into second grade. I can see up Uncle Sol's nose. He clips his nose hairs with a special scissors. He doesn't look like Daddy even if they are brothers. His nose and mouth are small and his eyes blue. Mommy says he doesn't even look Jewish. Daddy has a big nose, big brown eyes, and big, bushy eyebrows. His voice is big too, and he yells a lot.

Mommy makes me go to bed. I push my face into the pillow and close my eyes, but I can still hear Daddy shouting that Hitler is going to take over all of Europe if Stalin doesn't beat him to it. Hitler is the German and a Nazi. Stalin is the Russian and a Communist. Both are bad.

"Why would anyone go back to Europe?" Daddy yells. "I couldn't get out of there fast enough. And *now?* When they're herding Jews off the streets in Berlin? Burning their businesses? Don't you see, it's just the beginning."

He wants everyone to come and live here: Uncle Sol and his wife, Aunt Lotte, and their niece Hanna. She's the

daughter of their dead sister who *died of beedease* when
Hanna was little. Last year, Hanna's father married
someone else and the wicked stepmother threw Hanna out
of the house.

My mother starts talking about Hanna, so I get out of
bed and go to the door to listen.

"That woman won't even let Hanna visit. Otto has to
meet her one night a week in a café," Mommy is saying.
"Lotte wrote me all about it. How can he do that, Sol? He
didn't fight for Hanna, his own daughter?"

"He was always a weak man," Uncle Sol says.

"I'm glad Hanna's living with you and Lotte," Daddy
says.

"Of course. Where was she to go? Seventeen and with
no home. But to tell you the truth Abe, it's not easy."

"You must stay in New York, Sol." Daddy says for the
third time tonight. He never says anything once and it's less
boring if you keep count. "We'll bring Lotte over and
Hanna too. But we have to do it soon while we still can."

"I'm not going to be a burden to you, Abe," says Uncle
Sol. "I'll sell the lace factory, so I can start over with some

17

capital. I don't want to become your poor relative from Riga."

"God damn it, Sol. This is no time to be proud."

"You worry too much. Remember, I lived through the last German occupation. The Germans respect good work and good workers. Not like those barbarians, the Russians, who want to take everything away from us."

"These are not *your* Germans. Hitler and his mob. Listen to the man, for God's sake. It's no secret. He wants to wipe us from the earth. Of course, you know what I think of the Communists. We got enough of them trying to bring down the system right here in America."

"Well, your niece Hanna doesn't agree. She's got a goyish boyfriend from the working class. She thinks Communism is the answer. And she isn't the only Jew who does."

I'm getting sleepy, so I go back to bed and pull the covers up to my chin. I don't care about Hitler or the Communists, but I do care about not having a mother and being thrown out of your own house by your stepmother. Daddy would never let that happen to me. He's scary sometimes because of the yelling, but he isn't weak like

Hanna's father, Uncle Otto. "Goyish" I know what that means. "Working class" I'm not sure.

We're going to drop Uncle Sol off at Daddy's factory, so Daddy can brag about what he did in America. I know all about that too. When the relatives in Michigan weren't nice to him, he moved to New York City. And before he had a big bakery of his own, he drove a horse and wagon and brought bread every morning to people in Brooklyn before the sun came up. That horse knew every stop on the route. If Daddy fell asleep, the horse would go to the right house and shake his head, so his bells would jingle and wake Daddy up.

Mommy drives the car and Uncle Sol sits next to her. Daddy's bakery is downtown in Manhattan, so we must cross the Brooklyn Bridge. The grown-ups are talking in the front seat and they aren't including me. I look at the *skyscrapers*. Such a good word, I wish I made it up. Uncle Sol doesn't think the tall buildings are anything special. Not even the Empire State. He didn't like that we rode the elevator with "all sorts of people." We took him to see the sights, but wherever we went, Uncle Sol kept brushing specks of dirt from his jacket and pants. We went to see the

Brooklyn Dodgers at Ebbets Field. Uncle Sol didn't like people getting up all the time for peanuts and hotdogs.

"So rude. So disrespectful to the ballplayers," he kept saying, even after Daddy laughed at him and told him a ball game isn't a concert. He sniffed and tucked the paper napkin under his shirt collar, so he wouldn't get mustard on his blue tie.

Uncle Sol was mad at Dr. Bialkin who lives across the hall because he came to see us in his shirtsleeves.

"He doesn't even shave and he calls himself a doctor?" Uncle Sol shook his head. "You can't tell who anyone is in this country. No one gives you a card." Uncle Sol keeps a black case with *calling cards* and gives one to everyone he meets. He makes a little bow from his waist each time. Daddy doesn't pay attention. I do. Mommy says I'm *observant*. She's right. I can see everything like a telescope on the observation deck at the top of the Empire State building.

We pull up the car to Daddy's bakery on East 3rd Street where his workers make the bread and rolls they sell in restaurants and grocery stores. Uncle Sol gets out and kisses me on both cheeks. He's going to come back for dinner with Daddy. Before we drive away, Daddy pulls himself onto the loading dock and gives us a box of sweet rolls to take home. The whole car smells like cinnamon all the way back to Brooklyn. Mommy parks in front of Indian Walk on Flatbush Avenue where we're going for new shoes, the lace-up kind for school, but also Mary-Janes. It's the end of summer, and I have to go back to school. To start second grade. I don't want vacation to end but it's going to anyway.

Children and their mothers are everywhere, and shoe boxes all over the place.

"Alice dear," Mommy says. She puts her arm around me and she smells like lemons. "I want to explain something. It's hard for your uncle to be here without Aunt Lotte. They found each other later in life. Aunt Lotte was divorced, and Uncle Sol was a dashing bachelor, a man about town. They have a great romance."

"A romance? Uncle Sol?" I don't believe it for a minute.

"Daddy is upset. He wants Uncle Sol to stay here and to send for Aunt Lotte, but your uncle is worried she won't be able to sell his lace factory and pack up alone. It isn't easy for women to manage these things by themselves."

21

"Aunt Lotte *is* beautiful."

"She is. She has blond hair and green eyes. And she dresses very stylishly."

Uncle Sol keeps Aunt Lotte's picture in his breast pocket. He sometimes pats the pocket like he wants to make sure she's still there. Once he pulled the picture out, looked at it a long time, and wiped his eyes with his handkerchief.

I take off my shoe and put my foot on the metal measuring plate. I only have a sock on and the plate is cold. The salesman gets on one knee to see if the shoe fits my foot like he's the prince in Cinderella and I'm Hanna and my stepmother makes me sit in the ashes.

"You have big feet for a little girl,' the salesman says.

"I know," I tell him. "I'm going to be tall."

When Daddy and Uncle Sol come home, they bring a loaf of challah bread from the bakery. Uncle Sol says he really likes what Daddy calls his 'place of business'. They 'talk shop' over dinner which is just boring. I tear off chunks of challah to soak up the pot roast gravy. My mother is busy in the kitchen and can't tell me to stop playing with my food. I'm not playing; I'm observing.

Challah pieces soak up gravy fast. Besides, even if I play with them, I always eat them.

"When you own a bakery, your family will never starve," Daddy told Uncle Herman from my mother's family. Uncle Herman delivers newspapers for the *Daily News*. I was playing house with Uncle Herman's kid, cousin Elaine, and I told her "If things get bad, your family will have newspapers to read but nothing to eat."

"Shut up, Alice," Elaine said. Elaine is three years older than me and my only girl cousin until Hanna. Now I have two, one from my mother's side and one from my father's.

My mother brings the fruit and tea and cookies. Uncle Sol pulls out his cigarette and holder from its leather case and pats his pockets for his lighter. My father gets red in the face and goes on what Mommy calls 'a rant'.

"You know, Alice, your clever Uncle Sol is going back to Riga next week. He thinks he has all the time in the world." Daddy keeps looking at me like he's talking to me, so I have to pretend I'm listening. "He thinks there will be peace in Latvia because Hitler told Stalin he will leave the Baltics alone. Uncle Sol believes this rubbish because he wants to." He's talking like Uncle Sol isn't sitting right next to him. He grabs my hand and pulls me to the world globe on its wooden stand near the desk. He pokes at pink Latvia, purple Lithuania, and orange Estonia, the Baltic States on the edge of the blue Baltic Sea.

"You see how small they are? What chance do they have?" He twirls the globe around so hard the wooden stand wobbles and almost falls over. Daddy glares back at Uncle Sol who sits smoking a cigarette from his long black and gold cigarette holder. Daddy leaves the world globe spinning.

"Hitler is already in Czechoslovakia. He'll attack Poland any day now."

"Believe me, Abe," Uncle Sol says. He sighs. His voice is quiet. "This isn't an easy decision. But I need time. I have to sell the business. Get my affairs in order. Try to understand my position."

"Well I'm bringing Hanna over as soon as I can get her out. I already filled out the papers."

"You're going to have your hands full with that one," Uncle Sol said.

They keep talking about Hanna and her boyfriend and all the bad meetings they go to.

"She's a rebel. A Socialist. Maybe, God forbid, a Communist." Uncle Sol says.

"Please stop," Mommy scolds them. "The child has had a hard life. Her mother dies and this Yetta won't let her live with them. She's probably looking for a community. Something to be part of."

"Hanna's no child. But maybe you're right, Frieda. We never had children, and we certainly don't know much about raising angry young girls."

"Why don't you play for us, darling," Daddy says.

"Yes, do play, Frieda." Uncle Sol says. "That was a delicious meal you made tonight."

Mommy pats her skirt, shakes her fingers out and touches the keyboard up and down like she's saying hello to the eighty-eight keys. Then she plays. It's Chopin's pretty waltz again. I make pointy-toes and dance around the coffee table. I raise my arms like the ballerina in Swan Lake, but Daddy and Uncle Sol aren't watching me. They're listening to Mommy. Uncle Sol's smoke curls around the waltz notes in the air. When the music stops, they clap.

"Beautiful. You're playing better than ever, dear." Daddy gives Mommy a kiss on the cheek.

"You know Alice," Uncle Sol says, "My city is filled with musicians and music-lovers. On a summer night like this, you can hear music from open windows…not from concert halls but from people's living rooms. Mozart and Beethoven. Bach and Chopin. Some day you will visit us, Alice. You will love the ancient buildings and cobblestone streets, the turrets, and the clock-tower. It's like out of one of your fairy tales. They call that part of Riga the Old City."

"Old city. Old ways," Daddy says.

"Admit it, Abe. Our Riga is beautiful." Uncle Sol keeps going, "and everyone in our family—in your family, Alice—is a musician. Our sister, may she rest in peace, was a fine pianist like your own mother. She was only one of two Jewish girls accepted into the Conservatory. Do you play the piano too? You're teaching her, aren't you Frieda?"

"She's waiting until I'm more mature. Until I have bigger hands and stronger fingers," I tell him before she can.

"And the patience to practice every single day," Mommy says like she always does. "But you know, Sol, Alice is a reader and she's becoming quite the writer. Just listen. Recite your poem for Uncle Sol, dear."

I jump up from the floor and stand in the curve of the big black piano. I fold my hands in front of me like a singer at a concert. "The Seasons," I start.

"In winter, the trees stand bare and cold

In spring, their leaves unfold

In summer, their leaves spread open to look up at the sky

In fall they change color, then crumple and die."

Everyone claps. Daddy plants one of his sloppy wet kisses on my cheek and I wipe it off with the back of my sleeve. "She's only six," Daddy says.

"Going on seven," I say.

"Beautiful, honey," Uncle Sol says. "You capture each season with a single image. That's a skill. And you have it. Ah, I am going to miss you, Alice. You made me very happy." He gives me a big hug and his cheek is wet from crying.

Uncle Sol walks up the gangplank and stands way up at the railing of the ocean liner. People are shoving and pushing us, but Daddy keeps the new movie camera on his shoulder. I wave and wave until my arm feels like it's going to fall off. Uncle Sol blows me a kiss and calls something down, but I can't hear what. The thick brown film whirs round and round inside the camera. Daddy's doing a movie of Uncle Sol's trip to New York that we can watch anytime we want.

"It will be a record," Daddy says. "Sol's visit to America, Summer, 1939." That's the label he will stick on the metal spool of film when he puts it with the other ones of my birthday parties and the Feldman Family picnics. Daddy shoves the camera into its leather case and clicks the metal locks fast and hard like he's mad.

The horn booms, smoke gushes out of the smokestacks, and Uncle Sol keeps smiling and waving until

the white hull moves into the black water, and he becomes
a dot, and then a nothing.

THE COUSIN FROM RIGA

Hanna rushes into my life like wind. She moves so fast you are always in her way. She spills her books and magazines in foreign languages on my shelves without saying "May I?" and sprays her perfume all over, so everything I have smells like Hanna. Her eyes are bright blue and her nose is a small hook just like a falcon's. Hanna is from Latvia like Daddy's brother Uncle Sol who came last year. He went back even though it isn't safe there anymore, but Hanna is going to stay in New York forever in my bedroom.

"Your cousin has had a hard life. You must be nice to her." Mommy says. "It's a big adjustment. Coming to America by herself. Eighteen and on her own. At least, she has family here."

I want to be kind to Hanna because her mom, Daddy's sister, died when Hanna was a little girl. And last year, Hanna's father married someone else and the wicked stepmother threw her out of the house like Cinderella.

Hanna had to live with Uncle Sol and Aunt Lotte. But Hanna doesn't seem helpless or sad. She's too busy. Mommy makes me go to bed by eight, but sometimes Hanna doesn't come home until way past dinner and her alarm clock goes off before the sun comes up. She puts her wooden skis on her shoulder and marches out the door to meet her friends at the bus station. The phone rings all the time and it's usually for Hanna. Hanna likes New York. She says it's exciting to be around people from so many countries speaking so many languages. Hanna speaks four: English, German, Russian, and Latvian. And she speaks to everyone. She's looking for a job.

"I don't want your father to support me," Hanna says.

Strange newspapers and magazines come to the door now: *PM, The New Masses, The Daily Worker.*

"Communist propaganda," Daddy shouts, throwing them onto the table in the foyer. He says he hopes his Brooklyn neighbors don't think the magazines are coming for *him,* a loyal American citizen.

"How much do they pay you?" Hanna asks Patty, the Irish woman who helps every Monday. No one talks about money like that. It sounds rude. And when Patty tells her,

Hanna says: "That's not enough. You work too hard. You must ask for more."

Patty keeps wiping the kitchen counter. I can't tell what she's thinking.

When Daddy yells at the dinner table, Hanna yells back. She even interrupts him. If he shakes his fork at her, she grabs his wrist and makes him put it down. My mother doesn't say anything, but looks like she wants to be some place Hanna isn't. I make a butter puddle in my mashed potatoes and go to a beach with gentle waves, but Hanna's words keep flashing like neon signs on Times Square: 'enslaved', 'the masses', 'revolution', 'capitalism', big new words, grown up and scary. Daddy throws down his napkin and leaves the table.

"It's all right, Abe," Mommy says, going after him. "She's young. She'll learn."

"Your father," Hanna says as if I know what she's talking about. "I'm sorry. I don't mean to upset Aunt Frieda who's so kind to me, but your father is a capitalist. What can I say, Alice? Politics is in our blood. Yours too, you know."

Now I'm almost eight, I can walk to school by myself. Mommy gives me a paper bag with five graham crackers, one to eat each block. But she won't let me roller skate or jump rope because I might hurt myself. She's usually right. Sometimes they ask me to be a *steady-ender,* the one who turns the rope. They tie the other end to a tree. My friends pump up and down so fast their legs are a blur. I sing along: "A, my name is Alice, and my husband's name is Al. We come from Alabama and we sell apples." Since my name really is Alice, everyone has to sing about me even if I don't jump rope. But Hanna lives without parents and without rules. Hanna even has a fiancé, a person you are going to marry. Hanna put his photograph on the table between our beds. Her fiancé has light eyes, wavy brown hair, and a nice smile. Hanna kisses the picture every night. It's like the movies.

One night, Hanna gets back early, turns on the lamp, and sits on the side of the bed filing her nails. She has pretty white hands, smaller than mine even though she's so much older. I put down my Bobbsey Twins book.

"Tell me about your fiancé. He's very handsome."

"You really want to know?"

"I like love stories."

"You're going to love ours. Sasha proposed before I left for New York. He took me to our favorite bench on the river just when the sun was setting, and he asked me to marry him. Very romantic. Like in a book." Hanna holds out her finger and the tiny diamond sparkles under the lamp.

"It's so pretty. More. I want to hear more."

"Well, we grew up in different worlds, but we have a lot in common. You know my mom died when I wasn't much older than you, but until I met Sasha, I never talked about it. It made everyone too sad. Especially my father. Sasha wants me to talk about everything. He's a construction worker, but he's more sensitive and understanding than any one in Uncle Sol and Aunt Lotte's fancy crowd. I'm going back to marry him. I told Uncle Abe when I got off the boat. I told them both. Your father and Uncle Sol."

"You're going back too? Like Uncle Sol? Daddy says it's dangerous."

"I can't stay. Sasha's in the Russian Army. He's going to have to fight the Germans. I can't be here, so far away.

We're going to beat them, these evil Nazis. History is on our side. You know about the Russian Revolution, don't you? It changed the world forever."

"I don't think so."

"Don't they teach you anything in these American schools?" Hanna snaps, but then she adds, "You're going to need my help, I can see that."

"Does Sasha kiss you?"

"Of course. Girls like to be kissed. So, will you some day." Hanna puts Sasha's photograph back on the night table and opens the closet door. Her blouses and jacket hang next to my plaid skirts. She picks the blouse with the frilly neckline. It's green and shows off her red hair. Hanna is going out for dinner with a friend.

I turn over and try to sleep. My mother and father peck each other like canaries, but real kisses fill the movie screen and make the music get loud. My mother never talks to me about any of this but leaves books around the living room, so I can find out without asking. I don't believe a word I read in those books. It's too disgusting. Hanna knows everything, but I'm afraid to ask her. I don't want her to think I'm dumb. It's bad enough I don't know anything about the Russian Revolution. I'm going to look it up in the Encyclopedia Britannica. My mother bought all twelve volumes from the man who sells it door to door. Mommy wants to make me as smart as possible.

"In Riga, you live with Uncle Sol. Do you like living with Uncle Sol?" I ask Hanna another night. I have to find the right time and ask fast before Hanna jumps up to do something else.

"What do you think?" Hanna says.

"I don't know."

"You met our uncle. He was here last year, wasn't he?"

"Uh huh."

"Sooo, think about it. Would you like to live with him?"

"I don't know."

"Fussy little man. She's nice, our beautiful Aunt Lotte, and they both try I guess, but they care too much about what people will think and what people will say. The Riga gossips. It's the capital of Latvia, but it's a small city and everyone knows everyone. Not like your New York. So cosmopolitan. People free to do what they like. Riga is provincial. But when I go back there this spring, I'll live with Sasha. That will give them something to talk about, won't it?"

"Oh, you're risking everything for love. I like that."

"Do you want to see Fantasia with me tomorrow night, Alice? Everybody is talking about Fantasia—it's Disney, animated nature with classical music. Even your mom won't mind. But she really needs to see you aren't a little kid anymore. You know and understand a lot more than they think."

"I do." I tell her. "My teacher says so too." I'm definitely going with Hanna to see Fantasia.

Hanna can't wait for her letters from Sasha and her father, Uncle Otto, but she goes into the bedroom to read them in private. We all wait for letters from Uncle Sol. The letters come on one sheet of pale blue paper that folds up into its own envelope. It's as thin as tissue paper. The mail takes a few weeks to get to New York City in the USA and so the news is old by the time we get it. Uncle Sol says everything is quiet in Riga, but business isn't good because he can't travel to Europe for supplies or find customers to buy his lace. Still, he and Aunt Lotte are all right. He's not happy Hanna is working in a factory packing gloves.

"'What kind of a country is it, that a cultured woman, a talented pianist who speaks four languages has to work like a common laborer?'" Daddy reads to us from Uncle Sol's letter.

Hanna's glad she has work. She wants to save up and get her own place. Mommy's Uncle Dave got Hanna the job. He works in a factory too. Hanna met him at a Feldman Family Meeting. Hanna loves the Feldmans. "So unpretentious," she says. I love them too, but I have to look up 'unpretentious'.

I pick up the mail when I come home from school and see the next letter from Uncle Sol first. The letter was opened and sealed again with red tape by some stranger. That night my father breaks the seal. Sentences have been smeared over with black ink. You can't read them even if you hold the letter up to the lamp.

"All that's left is 'How are you? We are fine.'" Daddy says. He drops the letter like it burned his fingers. "Censored, damn it! And when the Soviets take over, it will be a complete crackdown. I don't know if Sol will be able to write to us at all. He probably shouldn't anyway because they could go after him."

Hanna looks sad. There are no letters from Sasha.

Hanna walks back from the Church Ave subway station and turns the corner. There's 215 Linden Boulevard. She can still see it written in Aunt Frieda's beautiful, rounded script on the envelopes all those years she was growing up. She used to picture a grand avenue lined with linden trees like their own Brivebas Street in Riga. But Linden Boulevard is a fairly modest avenue in a middle-class neighborhood. And her uncle and aunt live in a six-story red brick building with fire escapes, not wrought iron balconies like the ones back home. She's been here almost five months and she's noticing less than she did when she came. Too busy thinking. Thinking and worrying. It's late May and still light at seven. The air brushes her shoulders like the first spring breezes off the Baltic. But in New York, the balmy season seems to lull people and make them even more oblivious to what's happening an ocean away. Hanna scours the papers and listens to each radio broadcast. She has to go back to Sasha and of course, to Papa. How she and Papa loved reading Pushkin by the fire, cooking together, taking long walks along the Daugava River, and playing the piano and the fiddle. Her papa isn't like Uncle Abe and Uncle Sol. He always cared more about ideas than money. So how could he marry that terrible Yetta? With such a mouth on her, it's no wonder she was still single at thirty-five. They couldn't even buy her a husband. Until Papa. Just so he could send Hanna to Riga University. She won't go. And Yetta's a bitch. Hanna's glad she told her off. But she has to go back to Papa. She'll give him the courage to leave that woman and he will give her his blessing to marry Sasha.

This trip to Manhattan, her second, had been discouraging. The first time the motherly woman at the consulate said it was impossible to book passage across the Atlantic anymore; the major lines had discontinued service and the shipping boats refused to take anyone who wasn't politically connected.

"I came in January with no problem," she had protested.

"Ah, but so much has happened since. It's too dangerous now, dear. You're lucky to have come when you did. Many wish they had. And you are Jewish." The woman, who clearly was not, looked at her with sympathy.

"But I have to get back to my father. He's alone. My mother died when I was a child." If the woman wanted to sympathize, she could give her good reason.

"I'm so sorry," the woman paused. "Let me see what I can do. Come back next week."

But this afternoon, the same woman spread a large map across the desk and with blue crayon traced the route Hanna would have to take. The only way would be through Alaska across the Pacific and then over land through Asia and Russia, a journey of many weeks and one obstacle after the other.

"I can get you the freighter across the Behring Straits, and it's even possible I can get you the rail tickets. But, if I were your father, I would tell you to stay. By the time you get to Latvia, Stalin will have invaded the Baltic States. That's what everyone is predicting. The rail system will be immobilized for civilian travel. And you? A woman traveling alone?" The woman shook her head when she folded the map and handed it to her. "Take it home. Study it. I hope you come to your senses."

She will speak to Uncle Abe tonight. She has saved almost enough money. She can fly the first part of the trip to Juneau, and then, she'll see.

"You're a foolish girl." Uncle Abe sets his glass of scotch on the coffee table. The open map slides to the floor.

"I'm not a girl. Don't patronize me." Hanna counters. "You're so busy weighing the costs and the benefits of everything. You think like a business man."

"That's bad? Only to you, that's bad."

"Please Hanna," urges Aunt Frieda. "Stay until things are better."

Hanna rolls the map into a baton and shakes it at her uncle before striding out of the room. She goes to the bedroom and closes the door carefully not to wake Alice. The bedside lamp is on, but the child remains asleep, her book on the floor. Uncle Abe and Aunt Frieda don't bother to lower their voices.

"She's stubborn," her uncle is saying.

"Have you noticed it runs in the family? And maybe Hanna's right. This *is* a hard life for her. She should be with her father and that fiancé of hers."

"Are you out of your mind? She'll never make it. We can't even get a letter through anymore."

Hanna pounds her pillow. She holds the photograph of Sasha to her chest and rocks herself back and forth. She's so alone here. Is it foolish to think she can get back? And if she doesn't, will she ever see Sasha or Papa again? She should never have come. But who can she talk to? They try, her uncle and aunt, they do try, but they don't understand. Everyone thinks she should just be grateful. She can't let them know how terribly hard this is, day after day, not hearing anything, not knowing. Hanna buries her sobs in the pillow.

She has absolutely no privacy in this place. She's a grown woman and she has to share a room with a child. She glances over at her young cousin, breathing evenly and innocently inches away, her arm flung over her head. Alice is full of questions, she wants to learn. But the child is so protected. So coddled. Like most American children, she's unprepared for life, for loss, and for hard choices. Hanna sits up, straightens the sheet, and stares into the dark. That blue crayon scrawled across half the world. Uncle Abe is right. Going back to Riga isn't possible any more. She'll

43

never make it. And if she's captured or killed, what good will she be to Sasha when the war is over.

That stifling summer, her uncle rents a farmhouse in the country. Hanna has the apartment almost entirely to herself. She takes hot baths morning and night, before and after she goes to work at the factory. The odors of camphor from the glove packaging still cling to her skin. It's Saturday. She spent the afternoon reading in Prospect Park and now she lingers longer than usual. She sinks into the tub, refilling it every few minutes. The steam rises again and again until Aunt Frieda's flowered wallpaper curls away at the seams. She holds her breath, slips under the water, counts. She pulls herself out of the tub, gasping for air, swings her legs over the side, towels herself lightly, and allows the air to cool her burning skin and dry the drops on her belly and between her fair breasts. She wraps a towel around her thick red hair. She's the only redhead in the family. When she was a child, she felt sure she had Viking blood and had been switched as a baby with some Swedish family.

Hanna pulls up a chair to the radio. As everyone warned, the Soviets swept into the Baltic States in June and now occupy Lithuania, Latvia, and Estonia. Sasha must have been called up already. No one trusts Hitler to keep the pact and stay out of the Baltics and the Ukraine. While she can linger in a hot bath in a country at peace, Sasha faces danger every day. The factory owners and the bourgeoisie, like Uncle Sol and Aunt Lotte, have good reason to hate the Soviets. But Sasha's family owns nothing. So, they will be fine. How do we get rid of this obsession with personal property? Aunt Lotte and Aunt Frieda know how to make a home beautiful. She has to admit she too likes pretty things. Someday, she'll have her own place with colorful pillows, small statues, and modern china. Just last week, she saw this fine white china at Altman's Department Store, the salt and pepper shakers shaped to wrap around each other like bodies.

Each weekend, Uncle Abe asks her to drive with him to the farm, but she likes to stay in the city and go out with her friends. During the week, he eats his dinner at the Automat, comes in late, snaps open his newspaper and says nothing to her. But tonight, Uncle Abe arrives early and holds out a shopping bag with a bowl of homemade Italian meatballs.

"My factory foreman, Tony Leone, brought these today. Would you believe, he made them himself? *He* made them. Not his wife." He eases the striped bowl out of the bag and slips off the rubber band that keeps the wax paper on top. "Tony even gave me a box of spaghetti in case we didn't have any." He sets the box on the kitchen counter. "And I brought a loaf of bread from the bakery. It's in that bag with the company name."

"Thanks, Uncle Abe. I only grabbed a sandwich for lunch." Hanna reaches for the cast iron saucepans, and Uncle Abe loosens his tie, rolls up the sleeves of his shirt and sits down at the kitchen counter. The meatballs begin simmering on the stove. Soon Hanna is pouring the boiling water and spaghetti into a colander. Uncle Abe opens a bottle of Chianti and gives them each a glass. "Fine dining at the Golds!" he says and tips his glass to hers.

"It's funny, Hanna. Tony knows I'm what he calls 'a summer bachelor,' and I can't convince him I like the food at the Automat. Nobody believes me, but the chicken pot pie is really good. What a great idea, the Automat...all those prepared dishes behind those little glass doors. You put a quarter in the slot and you get a dinner. Perfect for modern times with everyone too busy to cook. Some smart businessman thought that up. And this country made it possible for him to succeed." Uncle Abe takes every chance he can to praise free enterprise.

"Delicious," Hanna says. "You have to thank Tony for me." She wipes some sauce from her chin. The meatballs are almost too fragrant, too good.

"You can't get anything like this even in a good Italian restaurant. "

"Of course not. And Tony knows I love Italian food. He always brings me a dish if he has extra. I have an Irishman too, one of the truck drivers, who comes in with soda bread fairly often. I don't care for it, but I don't let him know. And I wear a green tie every St. Patrick's Day." Uncle Abe pats his barrel chest. The large white napkin he tucked under his crisp white shirt collar is spattered with sauce

"Your workers like you," Hanna finds herself saying. "I could tell that day I went to the bakery." Uncle Abe had greeted each of his workers by name, and had asked about wives and children. He had slipped a few bills into the hand of one man with a sick child, another whose daughter was getting married. "Your workers do like you."

But Uncle Abe doesn't seem to hear. "Oh Hanna," he says after a moment, "all I do is worry about Sol and Lotte and your father. And of course, Sasha too. Here we are sitting down to a good dinner and they probably don't even have enough to eat. We might have gotten all of you out in time. Your uncle wouldn't listen. And now they can't get through to us. Not a word for, what is it? Three months?"

"Three months, yes. Three months. And Sasha used to write every week."

"It's terrible. Terrible."

"You know, Uncle Abe, I was furious when Stalin signed the pact with Hitler last summer. Soviet doctrine welcomes people of all faiths and to make a pact with Hitler with his disgusting racial policies? I even broke with some of my friends over it." Hanna wants her uncle to see that although she often defends the Soviet Union, she's not uncritical.

"I'm glad to hear this, Hanna. Really glad. Forget doctrine. Stalin. Hitler. Doctrine is only an excuse for conquest. Stalin couldn't wait to pounce on the Baltics because he needs access to the sea. And Hitler gave him permission, at least for now. But your Uncle Sol kept seeing peaceful solutions. All I could see was two powers wanting more territory. It's only a matter of time before Hitler goes after the Russians. And then, it will be bad." He twirls the spaghetti around his fork absently and spears a last meatball. He pushes his chair away from the table fast and hard, so it scrapes against the linoleum floor.

Hanna begins to clear, and Uncle Abe actually gets up to help her.

"The Red Army will defend Latvia," she says. "Sasha talks of nothing else."

"Your Sasha sounds like a decent boy, and that's what they say. But believe me, Hanna, the Russians aren't really fighters. All bluster. No military discipline or training. Not like the Germans. Our poor nation is between a rock and a hard place. This is an American expression, Hanna, but it was made for Latvia. You know how I feel about the Soviets and I hate your Mr. Stalin, but Hitler? The Jews thought he was just crazy. That nobody would take him seriously. And look what's happening."

"I know. I know." Hanna sighs. She ate too fast and she feels too full.

"I guess only Hitler could bring us together, you and me." Abe turns and puts his large hand on Hanna's shoulder. "Just leave the pot to soak. And maybe you'll play for me tonight? That Schumann you were practicing the other day?"

Hanna is tired but she will play for her uncle.

TA DA!

I drag the Victrola on to the porch, put the big black disk on the turntable and the needle into the first groove. When I hear "The Hesitation Waltz," I run down the steps and lie on my side with my arms stretched above my head. I press my legs close together, and roll down the grass slope until it gets flat at the road. I push hard against the ground until the hill takes over and I can give myself to the downward pull, eyes shut tight, tumbling on my back and tummy over and over. The trick is to keep rolling as long as possible, and when the slope levels out, to push through the slowing down and stop at the bottom by the stonewall. You have to finish lying opposite the big stone house and not crooked half way. That's how I'm going to talk about rolling to anyone who wants to know.

This time it goes perfectly; I get up and wait for the spinning to stop. The grass leaves bright red stripes on my arms. Lawns look like velvet but they're prickly. You only find out by rolling.

We're living here in the country but just for the summer. Mr. Deanen, our "butter-and-egg man" gave us his house and moved into the rooms above the barn. Roosters wake us up and the cows get milked at the same time every day. A black and white puppy even comes with the house. His legs are wobbly and his bark is like a soft cough. When my cousin Elaine came last week, we put the puppy in a doll sweater and hat and pushed him in my doll carriage, but he jumped out and ran back to the barn. Me and Elaine went to the hen house and reached under the chickens. We pulled out the eggs, but the hens fluffed and clucked like they didn't like us doing that. The eggs felt warm from their bodies.

Daddy's car crunches into the driveway. *Ping, ping,* rap the stones against the tires.

"So how are my pretty girls," Daddy shouts. He pulls me and Mommy to his chest, tugs my braids, and kisses Mommy on her cheek. His white cotton shirt is soaked with sweat like a handkerchief with tears. 'Where does Abe get that energy?' people always ask. They want to find the place and grab some for themselves.

"There! Guess what's in my pocket?"

"Candies!"

"Oh, Abe. You'll spoil dinner."

"Spoil dinner? Impossible."

You can spoil a child, though. I'm spoiled. Because I'm an only child. People say Hitler is getting the *spoils* of war. *Spoil.* I say it over and over until it's just a sound with oil in it. Spilled oil because of the *sp.* You can light it with a match.

Mommy and Daddy go inside. The screen door bangs so hard it shudders twice. There's a deep line between Daddy's bushy eyebrows. I know that face. He's worrying about his brother Uncle Sol in Latvia. I sit on the porch steps, straighten out a long blade of grass between my thumbs and blow to make it whistle. I keep trying but I can't get the sound Daddy makes. Daddy reads the paper every day. I do too. The black headlines stretch across the front page and smudge your fingers. What will the newspaper write about when the war is over? Hitler is *committing atrocities* all over Europe. I looked it up in Webster's. My teacher puts pins in the world map to show us where this is happening. And Stalin? Well, Stalin marched into the Baltic States in June right before school ended. I'm the only one in class who knows where the Baltics are. No one has heard of Latvia.

Squawking and screeching explode from the barn. I get out of the kitchen before Mommy can swipe at me with her napkin. Even on a sunny morning, the cold night air stays inside the dark barn. Mr. Deanen chases a chicken. Sawdust scatters under his big brown boots. The scared creature tries to get through the open door and into the yard. Mr. Deanen grabs the chicken by the neck and sits down at the chopping block. The bird wrenches its body away, but its bright yellow legs and black toenails still dangle from his hand. Mr. Deanen takes the cleaver and chops off the chicken's head. Just like that. The head falls to one side, the beak stuck open in a loud kind of quiet. Blood spurts onto the block, splatters Mr. Deanen's apron like paint, and drips down to the sawdust. With one swoop, Mr. Deanen puts the headless chicken on the barn floor. It runs two or three steps trying to escape being dead, not alive anymore, but thinking it is. The bird falls over, twitches its legs once, and shrivels into a pile of feathers.

"You see, Alice. Chickens are as dumb dead as they are alive," says Mr. Deanen, looking up at me, his black moustache shining over his yellow teeth, like he's saying 'Ta da!' and expects me to clap for him.

I run back into the house. It's like my being there got Mr. Deanen to kill the chicken, but even worse, made the thing he killed seem stupid. I know they need chickens for food, but Mr. Deanen enjoyed the killing. People in Europe are being killed every day, especially Jewish people, like me, Mom and Dad, Uncle Sol, Bubbe and Zayde, and all the aunts, uncles, and cousins in the Feldman family. And those bad men in Europe, in Czechoslovakia and Poland, they enjoy the killing too. They make speeches and brag about it. Like they're saying 'Ta da!' I hear them on the radio and I see them in Movietone News. I won't tell anyone what happened in the barn. But every night before I fall asleep, I keep seeing that headless chicken trying to run faster than its death.

PROTECT OUR FREEDOMS

The stifling subway car careens towards the elevated tracks taking Hanna and her friends to the city beaches. Some in the crowd carry printed posters, others hold signs fresh off mimeograph machines in downtown offices. A few people credit The Committee to Defend America, the sponsor of the rally. Others, including Hanna's, flash Union insignias, like the ILGW, the International Ladies Garment Workers Union. Others claim socialist connections. But look, isn't this wonderful? Ordinary outraged New Yorkers are clutching hand-lettered cardboards: *Stop Hitler Now. Protect Our Freedoms.* The subway rattles above the ground and into the searing light of a July morning. Hanna, Zita, and Lisel beam at one another.

"Can you believe it?" Lisel says, "Look how many, Hanna. Everyone turned out." Lisel has family in Lithuania.

Hanna squeezes Lisel's hand. Lisel works as a maid on Park Avenue, but she lives on the lower East Side. Two weeks ago, Hanna moved into an apartment across the hall from Lisel. It's five flights up, a studio with a kitchenette, but it's the first place she can call her own in America.

Naturally, Zita snares one of the seats on the subway. A young man in work clothes jumps up as soon as she clings to the overhead strap and bends forward over his lap.

"Why thank you. How lovely of you," Zita murmurs, pretending she's surprised. And just watch her moves, why don't you? When the young man rises and Zita slides into his place, she brushes against his arm and lets him enjoy the milky white of her upper breasts. She crosses her legs, so her narrow skirt rides up her thighs. Her net gloves expose her delicate wrists. The few beads of perspiration on Zita's upper lip are the only sign it's brutally hot out.

Hanna met Zita on the boat coming over from Latvia. They held each other at the sound of each ship alarm. They worried about the mines. Zita may be pretty ignorant about politics, but when Hanna told her about the rally, she did manage to get up early enough to catch the bus in from New Jersey. Like Hanna, she has had no letters from her family in Riga for months.

They push forward towards the Rainbow Shell. Masses and masses of people cover the beachfront—there must be thousands—their excited voices drowning out the waves crashing on the shore. Lots of Mediterranean types, immigrants, most in work clothes, but here and there a seersucker suit and straw hat, a few blond and blue-eyed believers in the cause. Some have brought children. If her young cousin Alice weren't at summer camp, Hanna would have taken her to the rally. You can't expose kids too early. Hanna sees plenty of union placards bobbing in the crowd, and she looks for a familiar face from her local. She's shop steward at her glove factory and everyone is beginning to know her.

"Hey, Hanna," a voice calls out. She looks up into the moon face of Uncle Dave Feldman, one of the Feldman clan, her aunt's people. Uncle Dave got her the job packing gloves over a year ago. "I heard they made you shop steward. I told them you were one smart cookie. Good for you! And look who's with me." It's Dave's friend Leon Adelman, one of the guys in her shop, an older, experienced man. He nods at her.

"Great crowd, isn't it?" Leon takes a puff on his cigar. He's never without it even on the factory floor.

"Hi Uncle Dave. Hi Mr. Adelman. Come meet my friends." She's about to make introductions when the men are swept towards the band shell.

"Look. Look at that," Zita points. Two stuffed ostriches flank the entrance, each head buried in the sand. The sign on one says 'Lindbergh', the other, 'Wheeler'.

"I know Lindbergh, but who's this Wheeler?" Zita wants to know.

"A U.S. Senator. Senator Burton K. Wheeler. Lindbergh's buddy. They want the U.S. to stay out of the war," Hanna says. "I like the ostriches. Great photo op. It will make the papers."

"Take my picture," says Zita. She hands Hanna her brownie camera, throws an arm around the Lindbergh ostrich, and tosses her curly black hair to one side. "Another," she pleads. Lisel is tapping her foot and telling them they won't be able to see the speakers if they take much longer. Lisel is tall, thin, and very serious. Hanna met Lisel at some meeting, but they see each other at so many, she can't remember which one.

59

"This time I'll hold the sign and you can show it to your union friends," Zita is saying. She strikes another pose waving *Protect Our Freedoms.*

A man with a dark gray hat and a tie dangling from his open shirt collar rushes at them out of the crowd. He reaches into his pocket and flashes a press pass.

"Ben Rigby, *Daily News,*" he says to Zita. "Can I interview you and your friends?"

The others talk too long, but Hanna keeps the message short and gets in the name of her union and the local. Her people will be pleased.

"So, you all have family over there, right?" the reporter says, slipping his narrow notebook back into his pocket. His photographer takes their picture. "Hand on hip. A little leg. Flash those placards. You're perfect, girls. My editor's going to love you." The reporter grins. He gets them to sign permissions and gives them each his card before hurrying on. "Hey," he turns around, "come in with me. I can get you in front with the press." Naturally, he's got his eye on Zita.

"No thanks," Hanna says. "We're just fine."

"We'll catch you later and you can tell us all about it," Zita says. "You'll give us the *scoop*." Zita winks at Hanna. She loves American slang.

"I'll be watching out for you," the young man says.

"You sure know how to get attention, Zita." Hanna says. Zita is pulling a broad-brimmed straw hat out of her bag. She's fair and freckles easily. "Now if I could only persuade you to join your union."

"You didn't tell me politics was fun," Zita says, securing the hat and tying the strings. "You always make it seem so grim."

"It *is* pretty grim. Especially now. But I forgot how good you are. You could help. You *should* join your union." Zita works for a fashion designer. She makes more than any of them, but too little for what she does. What upsets Hanna is Zita doesn't even know she's being exploited as a worker and a woman.

"Do you think the interview and photo will make the paper?" Lisel asks when they get close enough to see the speakers massing on the platform.

"It's a good story," says Hanna. "Three pretty immigrants with relatives in countries invaded by Hitler? A natural. Unless something better comes along, they'll run it." She can't stand herself. Like it's all about getting publicity. She wishes she were someplace else, alone.

The boisterous crowd settles down. A glamorous woman in a fashionable pageboy crosses the stage. "I am proud to introduce Miss Tallulah Bankhead," they hear through the amplifiers.

"The movie star?" whispers Zita. "How come *she's* here? I love American movies, don't you? I do a double feature every Saturday."

"Tallulah Bankhead is very political. She supports us," Lisel says. "Her late father was Speaker in the House."

"What house?"

"The House of Representatives. The American Congress, Zita," Hanna says. "You have to start reading more than fashion magazines."

The famous star begins to speak in that familiar husky voice.

"Can you believe it?" says Lisel. "She actually sounds like that in person."

"This mortal enemy of every American principle is threatening us with the most destructive forces of evil ever to be visited upon mankind, in spite of what all the isolationists and appeasers are trying to hoodwink you into believing…"

Hanna likes what she hears. Very effective. Americans may not have the Hapsburgs, but they treat their movie stars like royalty. And then Edgar Ansel Mowrer. Good choice, too. The man was a correspondent posted to Germany and thrown out in the '30s. He knows there's no appeasing Hitler.

Supreme Court Justice Pecora is speaking too. He calls the America Firsters 'Wheelberghs'. That's going to stick. You need something catchy, something that makes every citizen feel like a Washington insider.

"I have a message to read from Secretary of the Navy, Knox," a voice booms out. "'The events of this summer may decide the future of America. Today, freedom and security have been crushed in Continental Europe. The British alone remain free. The Committee to Defend America is awakening the country. We must unite with lovers of liberty to fight for the preservation of the blessings of liberty for ourselves and for posterity.'" The voice echoes through the throngs and the crowd presses forward and roars.

A plane zooms overhead, a heavy buzz growing louder. A parachute drops and a huge American flag flutters down. Lisel gasps: "So moving!"

Over the loudspeaker: "I pledge allegiance…" All those voices chanting at once. Hanna joins in: "and to the Republic for which it stands. One nation…." Lisel's right. It *is* moving, but like Hanna is always telling the folks in her union, you have to wrap everything in the flag. This cause *is* patriotic. But most important, it has to *seem* patriotic. The other side always waves the flag. They say it's more American to stay out of the war in Europe. Hanna keeps learning how things work in this country.

The three young women drift back with the crowd towards the subway station, Hanna feels good. She was here. She did something.

"Hey," says Zita. "There's something funny about that school bus over there." She points to a standard yellow bus parked at the curb opposite the station.

"Maybe they brought a bunch of kids to the rally. It's certainly educational."

"I don't think so," Zita says. "There are blackout shades on all the windows. And I saw something like a flashbulb going off out the back window. Someone in there is photographing people in the crowd."

Hanna looks over at the bus. "Jeez. You're right, Zita. Sharp eyes. Do you think it could be the FBI, keeping track of us left-wingers? I heard that's what they do, but I didn't expect to be spied on at a peaceful rally."

"The FBI does it regularly," Lisel says with authority. "And the America Firsters work with them and are only too happy to smear anyone who wants the U.S. in the war."

"Really?" says Zita. "That's disgusting. I thought this was a country where you could speak out whatever you think."

Zita strides towards the school bus, pulls up her skirt to the thigh, and flashes her shapely leg at the back window. She shakes her placard, *Protect Our Freedoms*.

"Zita!" Hanna shouts. "What do you think you're doing?"

"I just want them to know their hard work isn't going unnoticed. Show your placard too, Hanna. Let them know they can't scare us." She yanks Hanna's arm. A flashbulb

65

goes off from the back of the bus. "I wanted a photo and we got one, didn't we? We even got one together!" Zita beams at her friend. Before Hanna can answer, someone calls out.

"What's going on, girls?" It's Leon Adelman from Hanna's factory coming out of the cigar store on the corner. Uncle Dave is right beside him, a fresh newspaper tucked under his arm.

"Great rally," he calls out. "Terrific turn out."

"See the school bus?" Hanna points. "Over there at the curb. Black out shades. They're taking pictures. Zita made sure they got both of us. I couldn't believe her! And I'm sure they just got you, Mr. Adelman."

Leon twirls his cigar and sniffs it. He lights up and takes a deep drag before he checks out the bus.

"Yup. Definitely FBI," he says. He touches his cheek. "I should have taken a closer shave this morning. They got photos of me from every angle. Hitler is slaughtering people, but you're suspect if you want the United States to get into the war. You're nothing but a Commie. Because now, we'd be coming to the defense of the Soviet Union." Leon flicks his lengthening ash to the pavement. "Let's get the hell out of here." He begins to cross the street for the train going back into the city, but Zita puts her hand on his forearm.

"What a minute, Mr. Adelman," she says. "This FBI. This is from the American government like you say? Who is this Hoover?" Her hat has slipped to the sidewalk. He picks the hat up, manages not to singe it, and hands it to her. She twirls it absently in her hand.

"The Federal Bureau of Investigation. J. Edgar Hoover is the head. Government funded, government sanctioned. You're a citizen, right, Zita? Well, they're using your tax dollars. They already got a big file on me. The FBI can make your life pretty bad if they want. Enough." He calls over to Uncle Dave. "Let's go already!"

But Zita is still looking at the school bus.

"I don't like this at all," she says to Hanna and Lisel.

"You were quite something, Zita. What got into you back there?" Hanna asks.

"I don't like spies, Hanna. People who rat people out. They can kill just like with bullets. I know. From what happened to my own family in Latvia, I know."

More and more people fill the street, but thousands remain on the beach. The rally will go on all night.

"Come on," Uncle Dave is calling to them. "If we miss the train, we'll have to wait at least half an hour for the next one."

"Hey there, Zita! I knew I'd have no trouble finding you." It's that Ben Rigby, the reporter from *The Daily News*. Zita rushes over to him and points out the school bus, but he just shakes his head. "Standard practice," the reporter says. "Come on, Zita. I want you to see some people who are really mad." He tucks Zita's hand under his elbow, but Zita persists.

"I don't get it. You're a reporter. Why aren't you going to write about these government spies? Why doesn't your guy take a photo of the bus? It's right here. It isn't going anywhere."

"Everyone knows about the FBI. I'm going to do much better. I can show you a mob who want the U.S. to stay the hell out of this war. Most are German Bundists. Some support Mussolini, the Italian dictator. Others are just professional haters. Gonna talk to as many of them as I can. Take some great shots. *That's* what I call news."

"But what about spying on U.S. citizens exercising their freedoms. Shouldn't people know about that?"

"I'm telling you, Zita, everyone knows," he shrugs. "And who am I going to talk to? You want me to rap on the door of a bus? Get my photo taken by the FBI? How is that going to help me? They'd just shut me down. Let's go, sweetie," he says, "Those people I'm taking you to are pretty worked up about the rally. Nasty folks. You'll see plenty."

"I do wanna see them. Hitler is murdering us, and they don't want the U.S. to stop him? What kind of people are they?" Zita says. And before Hanna can persuade her that this is a stupid idea, her friend is off down the street and back to the beaches.

Hanna, Lisel, and the two men climb the stairs to the elevated train. They just missed a train and the platform is empty. Hanna's worried. Zita always runs towards trouble. And that Ben Rigby won't be much help. He's building his own career and he has a pretty girl on the side? Well, why not? Newspaper men are notorious. She wishes Zita hadn't gone off with the guy and into that ugly crowd of America Firsters.

Hanna and Lisel grab a bench and prepare for a long wait. More and more demonstrators from the rally are beginning to crowd around them. Lisel and Leon Adelman keep talking about the FBI, but Uncle Dave comes up alongside Hanna. His brow is drenched with sweat and he's breathing heavily. It's been a long, hot day for a fat man.

"You missed the last Feldman family meeting, Hanna," he says.

"I don't live with Uncle Abe and Aunt Frieda now. I got my own place," Hanna says. "I thought you knew."

"And a shop steward too. Thank God, Abe got you out in time. You got a big future."

"Unions are the only way," Hanna says. "But you know all about that, Uncle Dave."

A screech of brakes. The crowd on the platform pushes into the cars. Hanna and Uncle Dave are pressed against the closing doors. Lisel is holding on to the pole in the center of the car.

"My people on Park Avenue—they came from Vienna in 1938—well they say this country is so obsessed with the Soviets, they're letting the Nazis take whatever they want. They only hope the Germans destroy Russia."

"Those folks you work for are right. And Hoover is going to go after Commies over here wherever he can find them. And even if they aren't Commies, just people who believe in justice, in a fair shake for the working man, he'll go after them and call them Commies." And Leon Adelman is off again.

Hanna waits until morning to call Zita's aunt in New Jersey. She doesn't want to worry the woman, but she's concerned she hasn't heard anything. According to the aunt, Zita hasn't returned.

"I thought she stayed over with you, Hanna."

"I'm sure she's fine. You know, Zita. She's a free spirit."

"She certainly is," says the aunt.

Hanna fishes in her purse, finds the card the reporter gave her and dials the number. It's legit. There is a Ben Rigby and he does work for *The Daily News*, but Mr. Rigby isn't in this morning. Hanna leaves a message. She's getting more and more agitated, furious with Zita for turning a positive group action into something about *her*. Hanna fumbles with her keys and starts to leave her apartment, but then calls in to work and says she'll be late. She needs to stay by the phone in case Zita calls. Naturally, Zita has no idea where Hanna works. Should she call the police and report Zita missing? But she knows how the police operate. They won't do anything for forty-eight hours, and then they'll tell you she's probably with her boyfriend, as if that's the only possible explanation for a young woman who is missing.

The phone call comes around eleven. Zita is whimpering, her speech slow and slurred.

"Hanna? Is that you, Hanna?"

"Are you all right?"

"No. I'm not all right. I'm in the hospital."

"Oh my God. Where? I'll be right over." It's King's County. Hanna sometimes goes to the children's ward to play music, but otherwise, never. What happened to Zita must be very bad to land her in the hospital. That Ben Rigby was entirely too slick and too practiced. And Zita— well, Zita is just naïve.

Zita's beautiful forehead is wrapped in gauze, her left eye black and blue and very swollen, her lips red and puffy. Hanna rushes over to the hospital bed.

"What happened? What did that guy do to you?"

"Terrible. Terrible people." Zita mumbles through her fat lips. She tries to sit up but falls back again. The bruise on her cheek is raw and red.

"It's OK, Zita. If it's too hard to talk…don't. You can tell me later." She takes a glass of water, bends the flexible straw and tilts it towards Zita's unrecognizable mouth.

Zita's speech is slow and labored. Hanna has to lean in to hear.

"Nasty people shouting and dressed nice. These guys punch Ben and knock him down. They kept kicking him. They dragged me to the beach. It was awful…." She stops and puts a hand to her face.

"My God…how horrible, Zita."

Zita falls back on the bed and tears run down her cheeks. "It was…"

Hanna gives her a Kleenex from the box on the table and she blows her nose.

"I must look terrible." Zita stops. "I asked for a mirror, but the nurse said they didn't have one."

A nurse's aide comes in with a tray of food. Chicken. Mashed potatoes. Peas. Zita pushes it away. Hanna reaches over and holds Zita's hand between her own. Those delicate net gloves Zita was wearing on the train—the flirtatious net gloves. Gone. Zita wants to tell her more. And then…slow and halting it all comes out.

"The big one pushed me down and called me a dirty Jew. He and his friend, a little blond guy dragged me to the beach and…did this to me. They punched me and I couldn't…." She begins to run her fingers through her curly hair, now matted with sand and sweat.

"Fucking Jew…he kept saying. 'Just look at her.' I still had the placard sticking out of my coat pocket. 'You want freedoms, Jew?' He said, the big one said, 'I'll give you freedom…freedom to go back where you came from.'"

"Bastards!" Hanna raises her voice.

"I fought. I fought. But…they wouldn't stop. I bashed my purse on the head of the small one, but he grabbed it and ran away with everything. They're terrible, Hanna, these what do you call them—America Firsters—these American anti-Semites." Zita begins to shake.

"Oh Zita. I'm so sorry. I wish I had been there with you."

"Why? So, they could beat you up? Another dirty Jew! I'll live. I have a concussion. The doctor says I'll have a scar over my eyebrow. That's OK. I don't want to forget."

"How did you get here?"

"Ben called the police. The poor guy was really hurt, but he held my hand in the ambulance. He felt so bad." She gives Hanna a faint smile. One of her teeth is badly cracked and there's a hole where another should be. She reaches over and squeezes Hanna's hand. "They tell me I'll be getting out tomorrow or the next day. So Hanna, I need to know. When's our next rally?"

Hanna bends to kiss Zita's moist cheek. She smells like medicine.

"And you know, that Ben Rigby?" Zita says. The old lilt creeps into her voice. "He acts tough but he's kind. He tried to take care of me. And I did give him a hell of a story. I want to get to know Ben better." She stops and holds out her hand as if to examine her fingernails. "Yes, I think I'll be seeing him."

LILACS

My cousin Milty pulls the lilac branch down. The petals tickle sweetness in my nose. It feels a little like drowning but in a good way. It's spring again in Benji's backyard. Benji is my cousin Milty's best friend. The house he lives in is a Home-Sweet-Home with a slanty roof, a front porch, and a backyard filled with lilac bushes. It looks like the houses kids draw in kindergarten. I live in an apartment building a few blocks away, but no one would want to draw it. We're in Flatbush, in Brooklyn. At least, we are for now. That's in New York City, New York State, the United States, the World, the Universe.

The lilacs are bouncing back into their bush. Benji runs at Milty and goes *pow, pow*. They crouch and point gun-fingers at each other. Bullet pebbles fly down the path. Milty is skinny and blond and doesn't talk much. Benji talks more and sometimes he pokes me in my tummy and grins. I don't like it when he does that, but Benji can be fun. One of his big front teeth grows over the other one so he looks like a cartoon beaver. My mom says he needs braces, but he won't get them because his mom doesn't have the money. My cousin Milty and his friend Benji are sixteen. I'm nine and Milty sometimes takes care of me when my mom has things to do. His mom, my Aunt Mildred, and my mom are sisters. Today, Mom is doing things for when we move. To Manhattan. She says I don't have to talk or think about it until September, when school starts. And I'm not. I'm not thinking about it. Ever.

I sit on a rock in Benji's backyard. When I close my eyes, the sun makes everything red. This winter the sun didn't come out for forever. It snowed and snowed in Brooklyn. Me and my cousin Elaine, Milty's sister, built an igloo on the curb right in front of our building, a real snow cave. We put a big piece of cardboard on the floor. And it stayed so cold that we crawled into the igloo after school every single day for over a week. With flashlights. Like Eskimos or snow queens. You can't do that in Manhattan with all those big stores. And Elaine gets to stay in Brooklyn. I'm squeezing my eyes tight, and I'm seeing even more red. Blood red.

"Don't fall asleep, Alice," Milty says. "We have to go."
He shakes my arm.

Me, Milty, and Benji cross the street to Milty's house.
We climb the stoop and he unlocks the front door. Then,
it's up the steep staircase, past the dark at the landing, and
to the front where his room is. Elaine isn't here today for
some reason. Model airplanes hang from Milty's ceiling on
white sewing thread. Milty keeps the window open and lets
them shiver in the air. Some go up, some lie flat, and some
are going to land on Milty's desk. Milty glues pieces of
balsa wood together so each plane looks like the picture on
the cardboard box. He paints them with a tiny brush to
make brown and green splotches or streaks of silver and
white. That glue really stinks. It makes my eyes run and my
chest ache. Milty lifts me up to touch the planes.

"Gently, Alice," he says. "Easy. Easy." The planes send
out bursts of glue like gunfire. It mixes with the B.O. smell
from Milty's bed. He never makes his bed and his mom
doesn't either. Mom says I'm too young to have B.O., but I
sniff every night to check. Benji bunches the spread down
to the bottom, and we sit on the crumpled-up sheets. Milty
starts to name the planes.

"Come on," Benji says. "Alice doesn't care about planes, do you Alice?"

"Go on, Milty." I say. "I want to know all the German ones. It helps the war effort." I stick my tongue out at Benji.

When he grows up, Milty is going to be an 'aeronautical engineer'. He'll get to fly a real plane into 'the wide blue yonder'. All us kids know the Coast Guard and Navy songs and the Marine hymn, but the Air Corps' is the best.

"Off we go into the wide blue yonder/Off we go into the sun…" I get louder and louder at the end just like the boys do until what my mom calls a *crescendo*. "We live in fame/Or go down in flames/Nothing can stop the Army Air Corps." When I slick my hair back behind my ears and look at myself in the bathroom mirror, my jaw is square, and my chest is flat. I could be a boy. But Benji told me I sing the song wrong.

"It's not *wide* blue yonder, Alice," he said. "It's '*wild* blue yonder'." I like *wide* better so I'm keeping it.

The boys are telling me I have to nap.

"I don't nap. You think I'm a baby?"

"Your mom says you have to," says Benji. "It says so right here on this paper." He points to his open hand. There's nothing there.

"Stop it, Benji," Milty says. "Benji and me have stuff to do, Alice." He pats his bed. "We'll be back. You want Archie and Veronica?" My mom won't let me have comic books and I have to wait until I come here where they have piles and never throw them out. At Milty's house, nobody cares if I read comics all day. I won't get to read them ever after we move to Manhattan.

"Milk and cookies," Milty is yelling from the door of his room. Benji is right next to him, grinning. "I read ten comic books," I tell them.

"Good for you," says Milty.

"I bet you read just the girly ones," says Benji at the same time.

"Nope. I like them all."

We go back to Benji's yard with a glass bottle of milk, three paper Dixie cups, and a package of Oreos.

"It's a picnic, Alice," says Benji

"I know that." Anything you eat outside is a picnic.

Milty sniffs the milk and says it hasn't turned. The milkman brings his mom two glass bottles once a week and leaves them at the front door. We sit on the bench with me in the middle, and we make faces with our milk moustaches. Milty gets tired of it and starts bouncing his ball on the path to the fence.

I stick a finger into the white Oreo stuff and zoom towards Benji's shirt like a plane, but he grabs my finger, puts it in his mouth, and licks it off. He pushes my hand down on the bench.

"You have pudgy fingers, girlie. Sweet baby fat," Benji says. He presses each finger until it turns first white, then red. "You're a round, juicy thing." He drops my hand like he doesn't like it anymore. But he looks at me hard. "You know, you really *are* pretty juicy, Alice."

"I yam. That's what I yam," I say. I want him to stop and I want him to play.

Benji pushes his Dodger cap way back on his head over his curly hair. A drop of sweat rolls down his cheek and makes a streak where the dirt was. He growls and opens his mouth so wide I see past his beaver teeth to the little pink skin hanging in the back of his throat. He burps deep, milk and chocolate. Milk coming up doesn't taste or smell like milk going down. It's getting dark and the lilacs are sucking up all the air. I could faint like ladies did, like Aunt Bertha did right in our kitchen from breathing boiled cabbage. I saw her go down, just like that. It was lucky she didn't hit her head on the table.

Milty is bouncing a pink Spalding ball he calls a 'spaldeen' high off the path. He's talking like a radio announcer: "He's got a bead on it. He's under it. He's got it," he says over and over. He throws the ball to Benji.

"Naw, not now, Milty," Benji says, like he's too old for catch. He goes to sit in the big wooden chair near the lilac bushes.

"It's getting dark," I tell Milty, but he just keeps tossing the ball at the wooden fence. It leaves gray smudges. Bounce. Smudge. Bounce. Smudge. I could not be here for all he cares.

"I like your lilacs," I call out to Benji.

"You can smell them better over here," Benji says. I go to Benji by the bushes. When I'm next to him, I breathe just lilac air with nothing else mixed in.

Benji grabs me and pulls me onto his bony knees. His breath blows wet and warm into my neck. He starts tickling me. It feels good but then it doesn't.

"Oh Alice, my juicy little Alice," he says in my ear.

"Let me go, Benj!" I cry out. "Milty tell him to stop." Milty drops his ball and comes running.

"Cut it out, Benji!"

"All right. All right…You're the boss." Benji says. He picks up his hands like he's under arrest.

I run out of the yard and down the path on the side of the house. I knock the garbage pail over; the lid clanks off and the can stinks like a sewer. I look both ways and run across the street to Milty's. The door is locked. Milty has the key on a chain around his neck. I sit down on the cold top step of the stoop. My mom still won't let me walk home from Milty's by myself even though I know how and I've been crossing streets since second grade.

Benji comes around the side of the house. His white shirt hangs out the front of his pants. "You know, Alice. You are really getting to be a tease." he shouts at me and he goes inside. The screen door keeps banging back and forth, back and forth. And here's Milty running up the stoop steps. He's pushing a bunch of those sickly, sweet lilacs into my face.

"Here, Alice." My stupid cousin Milty is saying. "Take them home and give them to your mom."

THEY LIKED MILTY BETTER

Sometimes Elaine and I start with Twinkie, the canary who keeled over and died from inhaling honey wine our grandmother fermented for at least a month before Passover. She called it *med*, but it was spelled mead. The fumes filled the house for so long nobody noticed them until they killed the bird. Twinkie was Elaine's pet and she felt terrible when it happened, that poor bird lying stiff as a yellow stick on the sandpaper floor of his cage.

Passover is coming soon and so after wishing each other a good one, my cousin Elaine and I are at it again, talking about what it was like to grow up together more than fifty years ago. Elaine lives in California and I live in New York City and we see each other every couple of years, but whenever we get going on the telephone, we're girls. I grew up with Elaine, her brother Milty, and lots of other cousins, mostly boys. I bring Elaine all the news from the East Coast where almost everyone in our family still lives.

"Remember when Cousin Seymour married the hippie folksinger? You know, she died a year ago," I tell her.

"Didn't survive open-heart surgery. Supposed to be routine, but there you go. And Cousin Seymour was asking about you, Elaine. He lives in Northampton, Massachusetts and has a heart condition, but he wondered if you want to visit him."

"Really?"

"Uh huh. I told him you lived in California near your daughter and it would be hard for you to get there. And you know what he said? He said, 'I always liked Elaine.' I think he still has a thing for you." Elaine has beautiful green eyes flecked with brown, a great smile, and terrific legs.

"Seymour wasn't bad looking."

"And brilliant with a degree in physics. He did research at Harvard."

"How old is cousin Seymour?" Elaine asks me.

"I guess close to eighty. And not well."

"Please make my excuses to him. So, I want to tell you, I found a recipe for mead. Do you want to try it?"

"Send it to me. The kids are coming, and we don't have a canary."

I get a special ceramic jug to help the fermentation. I wait three weeks then I call Elaine.

"I tried the recipe for honey wine. But it has no smell at all, and I just tasted it and it's terrible. It tastes like sour water and I don't think it's going to improve with time. One more tradition we can't revive. Whatever secret Bubbe had, she died with it."

"Did you know I was the one who found Zayde dead?" Elaine says. Bubbe and Zayde, our grandmother and grandfather, lived with Elaine's family. Of course, I knew about her finding Zayde, but I let her tell me again. We all repeat ourselves these days, but since we also forget what everyone says, it's not so terrible.

"I went into their bedroom. I was just a kid. I was supposed to wake him up and he wouldn't wake up. He had a history book on his lap. It was awful. I'd never seen a dead person before."

"You know the last time I went to our cemetery plot, I checked the dates on Zayde's footstone. He was only sixty-five, younger than we are now."

"He seemed so old."

"He was always old. I never liked it that he kissed us on the lips. He had a moustache and his cheek was scratchy like he didn't shave well. I don't remember much else about him," I say.

"I just think of him dead. Do you remember..." Elaine starts up again.

But I don't want to remember. I want to *be* there.

Elaine's dad, Uncle Herman, works nights delivering newspapers, so he's around all day in the bedroom with the shades drawn, lying on sweaty, smelly sheets, and listening to his baseball games. I don't know anything about the Brooklyn Dodgers, but I love their names: Dixie Walker, Peewee Reese, Duke Snyder and, best of all, Cookie Lavagetto. Over the radio, you can hear the crack of the bat and the announcer saying, "He's under it. He's got a bead on it. He's got it."

Uncle Herman is bald and when he's upset about a bad play, he runs his hands over his bare head and mumbles to himself. When my mom drops me off there after school, Bubbe is screwing the big iron grinder to the kitchen table to make gefilte fish. She uses three different fishes and grinds them together, cranking so hard the flesh on her upper arm jiggles.

"Can I help?" Elaine asks. But her mom, my Aunt Mildred, tells her not to get in the way.

"If you want to be helpful Elaine, you can bring a plate to your brother."

Elaine's brother, my cousin Milty, is seventeen, four years older than Elaine and seven years older than me. He never comes into the kitchen. He can't be disturbed. He's king around here.

Aunt Mildred heaps chicken, mashed potatoes, and green beans on a plate and hands it to Elaine without looking at her. Then she says, "wait, wait…" and smears some chicken fat on a piece of matzoh to add it to the plate. I go with Elaine because we do stuff together.

Elaine has her hands full, so I knock on Milty's door. No answer. I knock again, hard enough to hurt my knuckles.

"Whaddya want?"

"Dinner." Elaine calls.

"Leave it on the floor," Milty says. "I'm busy."

"It's going to get cold."

"Go away, bitch."

We go into the living room with our matzohs and chicken fat. There's plastic covers over the sofa and chairs so we can't mess anything up. Crunch and slide. Perfect food.

"Did Milty call you a bitch?" I ask Elaine.

"That's what he calls me."

"And your mom doesn't stop him or wash his mouth out with soap?"

"Naw. She thinks he can't do anything wrong. Because he's the boy. He's going to Brooklyn College in September."

"Not the Air Force?"

"Naw. Our big hero is 4F—that's what the draft board says. Would you believe Milty has flat feet? Gotta sit out the war. He's really mad and Mom's happy."

"You going to go to college, Elaine?"

"Naw. Mom says boys don't like girls who are too smart."

Aunt Mildred comes in wiping her hands on her apron.

"Gotta take a load off," she says. "You doin' all right there? Get enough to eat?"

But before I can say yes thank you, she starts with, "That son of mine is some kid," and it's blah blah blah about Milty.

"My Milty can put anything together. The radio was broken for days until Milty got hold of it." The boy has 'golden' hands, Mama says. "And our neighbor Jake is over here all the time asking Milty to fix his carburetor. I don't even know what it is, but my gifted son!"

"You talkin' about me, Ma?" Milty is in the doorway, tucking his shirt into his army pants like he just rolled out of bed.

"He graces us with his presence." Elaine says. Milty goes over to Elaine and grabs the last piece of matzoh and chicken fat.

"Hey, cut it out," Elaine says.

"You had plenty, Elaine," Aunt Mildred tells her. "Milty's skinny."

"You going to college in the fall?" I ask Milty. He can be nice to me because I'm not his sister. I want him to like me better than he likes Elaine.

"Yup." Milty tells me. "Gonna be an aeronautical engineer. The only guy on the airfield who knows how to fix the equipment. The pilot just drives the bus."

"Too bad he keeps flunking algebra," Elaine mutters.

"What did you say?" Milty asks.

"Nothing."

"Milty needs teachers that challenge him, or he gets bored," Aunt Mildred says.

"Whatever you say, Ma," Milty gives her a kiss and leaves a shiny spot on her cheek from the chicken fat.

"Your cousin Milty is going to take care of me and Uncle Herman in our old age."

"I don't know why you're not going to college too," I say to Elaine when we're sitting on her bed together. "You always get A's. Bubbe thinks you're really smart. I heard her tell my mom."

"I'm so glad Bubbe lives with us. She took me on a march for the rights of women. Did you know our grandmother marched so women could get the vote? Can you believe that only happened a little more than twenty years ago? When we marched down Second Avenue,

Bubbe had a blue banner across her chest that said,
'Workmen's Circle Women's Auxiliary'."

"You think I could come with you next time?" I ask.

"Bubbe tries to make it better for me. But my mom
says there's no money for me to go to college anyway.
When I get out of high school, I'm supposed to get married
to someone rich. "

"Do you want to do that?"

"I don't know. But I'm moving out of here, that's for
sure."

When Elaine's eighteen, she gets a boyfriend. He's tall
and skinny and still has pimples on his chin. And he's
Jewish, even though he isn't rich. Everyone thinks it's time
Elaine got married, but she breaks up with her boyfriend
and Aunt Mildred is hardly speaking to her.

Milty dropped out of Brooklyn College. He works in a
plant putting motors together. Aunt Mildred won't let on,
but Bubbe says Aunt Mildred's "*s'appointed.*" We love the
way she says that. Aunt Mildred doesn't talk about what
happened to Milty. If she did, she'd make excuses for him,
Elaine says, like he had the wrong teachers or that they
broke his spirit, whatever that means.

93

"I got a job, Mom." Elaine is saying. Aunt Mildred is at the sink, doing dishes, and she doesn't answer. She just hands Elaine the dishtowel. Elaine takes it and starts wiping a big white plate. She gives it to me and I put it in the cabinet.

"I said I got a job."

"So? What do you want? A drum roll?"

"Well, it's in Manhattan and they're paying me fifteen dollars a week. It's with an advertising firm. I answered an ad and I went for the interview and they hired me."

"Fifteen dollars isn't bad pay these days. But you shouldn't have broken up with Bernie. Big mistake, Elaine. He had prospects."

"Mom. You aren't listening. I have a job. In Manhattan. When I save up enough, I'm moving out to the Village."

"Over my dead body. That's the trouble with you young women. The war did it. Men were away and women had too much freedom. You think it changed everything? You young women don't care about your reputations. Reputations still matter. You're my daughter and you are living right here until you get married." She turns on the water full force and the suds from the sink splash over the floor."

"What are you waiting for, Elaine? Get the mop."

Elaine grabs the mop from the broom closet and flings it on the floor. Suds and water splash everywhere. Aunt Mildred jumps back.

"Are you crazy?" she shouts.

"You're the one who's crazy. What's wrong with you, Ma? You should be happy for me. You should be proud you have a daughter who got a good job all on her own." She's so angry she's shaking.

Uncle Herman comes in, slips on the wet floor and grabs the counter to keep from falling. Aunt Mildred starts wailing as soon as she sees him.

"Elaine," Uncle Herman says. "Why are you upsetting your mother? Look at her. You're making her cry. What kind of a daughter does that to a loving mother?"

"Why don't you ever take my side, Daddy? I got a job."

"She wants to move out, Herman. Ungrateful girl! Tell her. Tell her what people are going to say."

"Elaine, you have to stop this fighting with your mother. I can't take it. Is it too much to ask for a little peace in my house? I work hard and I'm entitled to a little peace." He picks up the mop and gives it to Elaine. "And clean this mess up, right now." He glares at her and walks out. The next minute, the crowd at Ebbets Field starts yelling over the radio.

Elaine lets the mop drop onto the sudsy floor.

"You don't care about me. It doesn't matter to you what I do. And it never did."

"I care about you all right," says Aunt Mildred. "I care about what people are going to say about a girl who goes off at eighteen and gets her own apartment when she has perfectly good parents who love her."

"You have a hell of a way of showing it."

"I never said you weren't pretty, Elaine. And I tell everyone how neat you are. You keep your bedroom immaculate. No one can make hospital corners like you can. I don't know why you're always so angry."

"Oh, Ma. You really are hopeless." Elaine runs out of the kitchen to her tiny bedroom at the back of the house. Milty doesn't live in his big room overlooking the street anymore, but they would never give it to Elaine.

Elaine is moving to a studio walk-up on Morton Street in the West Village. Bubbe gives her the heavy brass candlesticks she brought over from Poland. She also slips her fifty dollars for the security deposit. While we're in Elaine's room stuffing clothes and shoes into boxes, Bubbe picks up the photograph of her and Zayde that Elaine is taking. "I wanna tell you, sweetie, I liked being married to Zayde," she says. "He brought a paycheck every week even with the strike. I'm not against marriage. But what happens if you divorce? What happens if he gets another woman? You know the poster—that Rosie factory worker where she puts her fist up? I love that poster. It says women can work and earn a living too. You are first in our family, Elaine. You are like, what they call them I learn in citizenship class, the pioneers. You are my granddaughter, the pioneer." She gives Elaine a hug and a kiss. Me too. She looks like everybody's grandmother, gray hair in a bun, round glasses, a dark blue dress down to her swollen ankles, but that's what she says and that's what she does.

After Elaine's friend piles the boxes into his truck, Aunt Mildred finally comes out of the bedroom, sniffling and wiping her eyes.

"You'll see," Bubbe says." It will be good for her. Also for you and Herman." Milty is working for Ford and out of the house, so Aunt Mildred and Uncle Herman can finally take it easy. I see my aunt and uncle less after Elaine leaves, but they do seem happier. Having kids at home must be hard on people. Also, the Dodgers are having a good year.

When you open the door to Elaine's apartment, you walk right into the main room because that's the only room. But it's on the top floor and sunny. Everyone in the Village is young. The war is over and they're getting jobs in fashion, in advertising, in publishing. Elaine takes me to coffee houses where we listen to folk singers' moan about working in the fields, in the mines, and on chain gangs. We're city people, the children of Eastern European immigrants, but we love these songs. The walls of Elaine's favorite coffee house are draped in green velvet, the chairs are wood and mismatched, and the tables covered with checkered cloths and chianti bottles stuffed with candles. We pull and stretch the candlewax and roll it into balls and rods. We sip our wine like two grown-up women.

"How's your job?"

"They love me. They're giving me a raise and a promotion. I'm traffic manager."

"Sounds like you keep cars moving, but that can't be it."

"I keep the production of ads going smoothly. I manage the flow of paper from one department to another, so I manage everyone, from the top brass to the guy who sorts the mail. I'm good at it. I can't believe what I learned on Ocean Avenue, watching her every move and trying to please her, being able to take her crap, paying court to Milty, even waking up my dad, turns out to be very useful in the workplace."

"You're smart. Bubbe always said so." Our grandmother died only a year after Elaine moved to Manhattan.

"To Bubbe!" We say. The chianti is raw and clears my sinuses.

"Any marriage prospects?" I ask Elaine in the singsong voice of an old relative.

"I'm kissing a lot of frogs."

"I'm going to college in September. You'll still see me, right?"

Elaine does so well she can afford a bigger apartment. Once a month, Aunt Mildred takes the subway into Manhattan.

"You'd think she was traveling to a foreign country. Like I should get her a passport. So, get this. I open the door—she's never seen the new place—and you know how nice it is and overlooking the Hudson—and you know what she says? 'Why would anyone want to live here? It's the docks. Where the relatives came off the boats from Europe.' 'That was a long time ago, Ma,' then she says 'Don't teach me my history, Elaine. I know history.'"

"You can't make this up," I tell Elaine. I'm in the phone booth in my college dorm but I'm also right there in Elaine's apartment with Aunt Mildred.

"Next, she's opening my refrigerator and saying I have too much cheese. She asks me if I've gone on one of those crazy new high protein diets. 'Those diets *are* crazy,' I tell her and she almost collapses from the shock. 'I think too much protein is probably not good for you.' 'You think so?' Ma says. 'Of course, you lose weight. But you gain it right back when you start eating everything again.' We talk about how much we love food in our family and how we all struggle to lose weight. It's a lovely moment even if it doesn't last long. Then it's on to Round Two. And she's at me again."

"'You know why you're not married, Elaine?' Mom says. 'I'll tell you why you're not married. It's because no man wants to marry *damaged goods*. Boys don't want a *fast* girl who's living on her own. They want a good girl who lives at home. When they pick her up, they can meet her mother and have a smoke with her dad.' She stays one hour. She tells the ladies on Eastern Parkway that I run an advertising firm. I'm not a partner yet, but I will be. She brags about me because it makes her look good but to my face, I'm nothing."

When Elaine is thirty-three, she calls about this guy she met. One of my kids is screaming and I have to call her back. I just turned thirty and I worked for a year after college and got married. My husband supports us. Sorry, Bubbe. At nap time, I make a strong cup of coffee and call Elaine.

"So?"

"Neal's a social worker. He works in VA hospitals all over the country. He's smart and nice. I used to think nice was boring. What's boring is neurotic. The neurotic ones seem exciting at first, but it's the same damn obsession over and over."

Neal wants Elaine to marry him and move to Wyoming. With her skills, she'll find work anywhere. He thinks putting some distance between her and her family would be a good idea.

"Do you think he's turning you against all of us?"

"Not *your* family. It's just—you know what I grew up with. I made the break. Neal wants me to feel less guilty about it."

"You think it's his training as a social worker?'

"Neal is a loving and understanding guy. This isn't a business deal: what *I* bring to the table, what *he* brings to the table, the way my mom sees marriage. This time I'm in love."

Elaine comes home whenever there's a crisis, a heart attack for her mom, her dad's bout with pneumonia, but she leaves as soon they don't need her. Milty picked a fight with his mom and dad years ago and stopped talking to Aunt Mildred and Uncle Herman altogether. He didn't come to their funerals.

The other day, Elaine and I were on the phone. She and Neal live in California.

"Do you ever hear from Milty?"

"Never. He's somewhere out west, Arizona I think. He's divorced. Has a grown son who won't have anything to do with him."

"I guess being the favorite didn't work for Milty," I say. "But look at you, Elaine. They treated you rotten and you did just fine."

"You really think so?" Elaine asks.

LIFE LIST

Eight people train their binoculars into the woods alongside the trail. They're searching for a four-inch bird. A ruby-crowned kinglet. Only a taxidermist will ever see the red spot on its head. Otherwise, the kinglet is unexceptional as far as Elaine can tell from the illustration in Peterson's, their guide to birds.

"There he is," says their leader, the naturalist. "Tall tree behind the cedar. Near the top. At one o'clock."

Everyone swivels. First, Elaine has to figure out which tree is a cedar. She's an urban person. Lives in Manhattan and works for an ad agency. The closest she gets to nature is when they're on set doing a commercial for hotdogs in a fake suburban backyard. Her current boyfriend, Tim, is a bird watcher.

"How did you get interested in birds?" a woman asked her last night. She came all the way from Texas to see a painted bunting. Elaine looked for the bird in Peterson's.

104

The bunting used up every Crayola in the box, and unlike the kinglet, does seem worth a detour.

"Love," She told the woman. "I'm doing it for love."

"I know what you mean." The woman tugged at the drawstring of her tan pants and tucked in a safari shirt made of parachute material.

Elaine didn't mention that last year she was going to the opera. Her old boyfriend was obsessed with Wagner.

"Opera tickets are expensive," Elaine's mother said, "so he must be making good money." She worries Elaine will never marry. She doesn't shut up about it either. Still, when Elaine's boyfriends take off, Elaine has more to show than a broken heart. She's a living compendium of their obsessions. You should hear her on basketball. She can even do old cars. But ironic distance isn't helping her get a life mate. It's like she's always wearing binoculars, watching the bird and watching herself watching the bird at the same time.

"You should live in the moment," one boyfriend urged her. Of course, Elaine had heard this before, but she was in love with him, so it sounded new. Feel my hand on your thigh. Live in this kiss. Welcome this strange tongue into your mouth. Meanwhile, she's thinking she's going to gag on this strange tongue. He thinks passion. She thinks invasion. It turns out most moments are pretty lousy. You wouldn't want to pay attention to them any more than was absolutely necessary.

By the time Elaine looks for the ruby-crowned kinglet, he isn't at one o'clock. He isn't even *on* the clock. The woman in the parachute material is already jotting down something in her notebook. She is keeping what people obsessed with birds call a "life list." They track every single bird they see. She's up to 238 different species, including every kind of sparrow (there are *kinds* of sparrow?) and every kind of duck. (ditto, ducks?) Once she's seen her ruby-crowned kinglet, she won't even *care* if she sees him again. And so far, the painted bunting has proven elusive.

"I got him," she calls out to Elaine.

"Good, good." Elaine's binoculars have only managed to enlarge the veins on the underside of a leaf. Tim slips his hand up her t-shirt and slides his fingers along her spine. "How you doing, Laney?" he asks. Elaine wants to wrap her arms around Tim's neck and nudge him towards the ground. But the one time they made love outdoors, the bed of moss turned out to be as rough as a scouring pad. Something sharp pressed against her ass. A black ant crawled up her underarm, headed for her armpit.

"If you close your eyes, we might as well be in bed," Tim had said to her back then. "Just open your eyes."

"I can't," she'd squinted up at him. "The sun's too bright."

"So. How you doing?" Tim repeats.

"Great," she tells him. "Just great."

He's such a pretty boy: black hair, blue eyes, lightly-freckled skin, like a laddie in an Irish ballad. Elaine has already added him to her life list. Her first Catholic. And even more satisfying, a species her mother hates.

The naturalist is moving them along the path to find the screech owl he saw last night. Tim presses on. But Elaine hangs back, slows down; the binoculars around her neck cease bouncing against her chest. Peterson's dangles from her hand, her forefinger stuck on the page with the kinglet.

It is late in the day when the woods shimmer in remembered light. Backlit, the leaves and branches splotch the trail with delicate design. Tim and the others have gone on ahead, but somehow, she wants to linger here alone. The fading sun pales against her skin. The tree trunks cast lengthening shadows. In a clearing, a clump of ferns finds a spotlight. The birds call out, their cries urgent, long whistlings and high trills, *weetchie, weetchie,* and *tsee, tsee, tsee.* Others sound like quick intakes of breath. She slows her own breathing to listen. The scent of honeysuckle floods the air. Wild azaleas burn through the gathering dark and dogwoods spread lace against the coming of night.

Elaine sinks down onto a fallen log, snaps Peterson's shut, and slides the binoculars into their case. The air freshens; a small brown bird hops from branch to branch and the leaves tremble after him. Incomprehensible sounds shift and change, passing on to the ridges beyond. An ant, single-minded, determined, drags a shred of grass across a mound of earth. The breeze reshuffles some dead leaves and they whirl and hover around her ankles before fluttering on. The night air hints at the chill to come. Elaine touches her cheek and feels the heat. Her palm comes away moist. It's all too much, but somehow, she thinks she may be ready.

PART TWO

HOME MOVIE

My mother died years ago, but I often imagine my way back to her. It's like making a home movie, even though the heavy strip of celluloid jerks through an ancient camera that is always breaking down.

Sometimes I can see a pram filling the small hallway of the apartment in Brooklyn where I grew up. A baby lies asleep swathed in blankets, a faint smile on her lips and spittle on her chin. That's me, little Alice. Four months old, fresh and pink. My mother trails a finger along my downy cheek. She removes her pearl hatpin and her blue cloche and hangs her fur-tried jacket in the closet, grasping the hanger so it won't rattle. She runs her hand along the pleats of her skirt, slipping off her shoes, straightening the seams of her stockings. Her movements are slow and deliberate as if she were already old. She shakes out her hair and touches her short brown bob. She cut off the girlish braid she used to wear when she climbed tenement stairs to teach piano to the children of immigrants. She had twenty-four students and made more than her father who drove a truck for Macy's.

Mom puts on pink slippers and heads for the kitchen. She hopes I'm drunk on summer air and will stay asleep and that my father won't come home from his bakery too early. He's fifteen years older and asked her to marry him only after he was sure of his success in America. My gentle mother warmed to the restless energy of this square jawed and explosive man. I'll grow up to be more like him than her.

She's making meatloaf tonight. Dad claims her meatloaf is almost as good as his bachelor portion at the Automat on Flatbush Avenue in Brooklyn, New York. For us, this Brooklyn is complete unto itself, our universe. There, on Linden Boulevard, my mother pushes my carriage under canopies of shade trees, feeling the milk surge through her breasts. With wide gray eyes, she watches the pollen shimmer down on the hood of my carriage.

"When I went into the hospital to have my baby, the trees were bare," my mother will tell everyone for years, "but when I came out carrying my daughter only ten days

111

later, the trees were covered with bright green buds. Spring was everywhere."

After tying the strings of her ruffled half-apron, my mother sets the kettle to boil and adjusts the blue flame, so it is exactly two inches from the mottled bottom. She lifts the mound of chopped meat from its heavy brown butcher paper, measures out the ingredients, and shapes the loaf into a pan. She turns the oven knob to start the gas flowing, strikes a match and checks to see that the burners below have caught fire. Then she sets the pan into a larger pan of the boiling water and places it carefully on the oven rack. She doesn't spill a drop.

Going back to the pram in the hallway, Mom releases the metal brake and rolls the carriage towards her to take off my pink sweater, slowly, gently. I'm flushed with the heat and give her a drowsy, grateful smile. Even at four-months-old, I'm a good child, willing to sleep away the entire afternoon to please her. She turns me on my tummy and tucks the light summer blanket around me. But my perfect mother has forgotten to lock the carriage. I want to call out, 'the brake, Mom. Pull down the brake!'

Her mind is elsewhere, seeking the quiet time ahead. Each afternoon during my longest nap, she practices the piano for two or three hours as she has every day of her life since childhood. She's moving towards the living room and her baby grand, pausing to inhale the rich smells from the kitchen, admire the pale gray sofa and fluff up a velvet pillow. She walks beyond the Steinway to the casement window, breathes in the fragrance of a summer afternoon, and runs her fingers along the sill, seeking flecks of dust. My father will have no complaints tonight—a beautiful clean home, a contented baby, and a meatloaf almost as good as the Automat's.

She pulls out the piano bench, smooths the knife-edge pleats of her skirt and touches the keyboard with her fingers as if in greeting. As usual, she starts with an etude, slowing the tempo to correct the fingering, leaning forward to the music rack, and penciling in the number 4 or 5 every few phrases, pausing only to brush the pink eraser specks from the keys, her rosebud mouth tight with concentration. Mom sets the metronome and plays the same piece with blocked chords, with dotted quarters, at a slow tempo and then fast. Across the years, I scan the scene and watch and listen as my mother works on her repertoire, while as a baby in the pram I remain asleep, her music entering my dreams for life.

The brake on the carriage is unlocked, the baby Alice, in danger. But my mother is thinking only of Carnegie Hall, where she often climbs to the highest balcony to hear great pianists like Josef Hoffman scatter the notes of Rachmaninoff like shooting stars. She begins the same Chopin waltz she assigned to a student preparing for Juilliard. When she came for the lesson, his mother said, "I luf dat piece you gif my son," and began to croon *"Die de diedle die de die,"* turning Chopin's elegiac opening into a plaintive Yiddish song. With empathetic mimicry, my mother will tell the story to my father. Then, after she serves dinner and washes the dishes, she will sit down at the piano and play for him.

Months before my father, Abe Gold, met my mother, he heard her practice through the wall they shared in her parents' apartment on the Lower East Side of New York City where he had rented a room. Dad came from a family of musicians and could whistle every melody. But when he married Frieda Feldman, he insisted she stop teaching.

114

Mom hoped to keep the student she was preparing for Juilliard, as well as a few of the more gifted, but he wouldn't let her. If she went to work, people would think he couldn't support a wife.

And now the baby in the pram, the baby Alice, wants to turn over. My little fists push down on the pink cotton sheet. My mother doesn't see or hear. I'm trying to flip onto my back. The shiny new carriage begins to roll and tip, its wheels slipping on the linoleum. I cry out, startled, about to be smashed beneath an overturned pram, my delicate fontanel crushed into tiny bits of bone.

"We were lucky I was working on a Bach prelude and not that noisy Liszt sonata," my mother will tell me years later, recalling that dreadful moment when she almost lost her only child.

"I heard you cry, rushed to the hallway and scooped you up just in time. I had tied the strap around you, yes, but you were dangling over the side and the carriage, that heavy, expensive carriage Dad insisted we buy, was about to topple over. It was terrible. I was so busy with my music I forgot I had a child. It's not as though I had any *reason* to practice so many hours every day."

"You were wonderful," I had assured her. "You practiced the piano for the love of it. And that's something you taught me."

I watch my mother cradling me as a baby in her arms, opening her blouse and easing her nipple between my lips. She wraps a shawl around me, goes to the window, and looks down into the street. Perhaps she's already thinking about her little Alice walking along the sidewalk below to school six blocks away, nibbling on the Graham cracker she gives me for each block, sitting on the curb with my friends as we talk to our dolls or tighten our roller skates with keys we hang from strings around our necks. She's already worrying that I will turn the corner out of sight and forget to look both ways for cars, or twist an ankle and scrape my knee in the school playground, and there will be nothing, absolutely nothing, she can do to keep me safe. But what must have worried her even more, I know now that I have a grown daughter of my own, is the harm she herself will cause. She'll forget to put the brake on the carriage, wrench my arm when she drags me from a tantrum in the grocery store, arrive late to pick me up after a lesson and slap my wrist when I strike the wrong notes at the keyboard. She

116

will try not to, but one day she will criticize my hair, my clothes, and my choice in men. She will also make me feel guilty for what I did or did not do.

"It's all right," I want to call out as she rocks me at the window, blaming herself for what almost happened. "You listened. You cared. You kept showing me how and where to find joy."

If only I could crawl beneath my mother's piano like I often did when I was a child. In that vaulted black and gold cave, I will watch her plump ankles depress the brass pedals once again, seek shelter beneath her cascading notes, and somehow find a way, even imagined and imperfect, she can get me through the sorrows and losses I know now are coming.

THE GARDEN CAFETERIA

"It's not that I don't love it," Frieda hesitates. "It just doesn't feel like home yet." She and Abe are having breakfast at the window overlooking Central Park. The morning light spills over the table and gilds the coffee cups. She doesn't know what's wrong with her, but since they moved here from Brooklyn, she has this vague sense of unease.

"Don't worry," Abe says, patting her hand. "We can afford an apartment on Central Park West."

"I guess it will just take me time to get used to…."

Alice rushes into the room with her schoolbag. Her new school is only a bus ride away, but she's often late. Abe peels off a bill from the roll in his pocket, hands it to his daughter, and gives her a hug.

"You know honey, I was just telling Mom the three of us might have to go to the poorhouse someday. Do you think you could do it?"

"Oh Daddy," Alice pulls free and rushes out the door.

"Bye, honey. Have a good day," Frieda calls after her.

"You have to stop saying that," Frieda scolds Abe. "It's not funny." This isn't the first time Abe threatened Alice with the poorhouse. He wants her to know they didn't always have money and could be broke again. But he also enjoys teasing. Frieda doesn't like that about him. Still, only an hour ago, they inaugurated the new bed with sweet morning love, teeth brushed and minty, his face closely shaven, a generous indulgence. He's generally left for the office by now.

On impulse, Frieda suggests they meet for lunch at the Garden Cafeteria downtown, only a few blocks from his commercial bakery and not far from the settlement house where she plays the piano. They used to meet for lunch regularly when Abe was starting his business. She misses those early days of hope and struggle.

"All right," Abe says reluctantly. "12:30. One hour. You know how hard it is for me to get away."

A chill in the air this November day. Frieda touches the mink scarf Abe insisted she have, and pulls down the brim of her green felt hat. It's a long walk to the subway station. Columbus Avenue. Then Amsterdam. Just as she reaches Broadway, the shoeshine boy slaps a rag on a shoe

119

again and again like a drummer, and the morning sun bounces off the stained-glass window of the church and lights a single patch of blue. The last three red leaves cling to the maple tree and remind her of that delicate line drawing she saw in the gallery last week. When she lingered over the drawing, the gallery owner came over.

"Beautiful, isn't it? Do you know his work?" He asked her. "Hugo Friedburg, a big name in Europe. Friedburg fled Vienna in 1937." What he meant was these people need our help, and why shouldn't compassion boost commerce? She'll ask Abe if she may buy the Friedburg drawing for the new apartment.

The subway car sways around a corner like an undulating snake and everyone opposite her sways in unison. Frieda pats her shopping bag with the Chopin mazurkas and the Schumann impromptus. The old people know every note. And afterwards, it will be lovely to eat at the Garden, a dairy restaurant in the old neighborhood where she grew up. In only a couple of years, the Garden has become a gathering place for Jewish intellectuals. Their contentious and heavily-accented conversations always remind her that despite the black-outs, the threat of bombs, the worries about relatives in Europe, the life of the mind is still alive and well in downtown Manhattan.

Sometimes, Frieda prefers people who don't call attention to themselves, who modulate their voices, and speak in pure, unaccented English when they discuss politics and literature, art, and music. They always behave as though they're in agreement, even when they aren't. She has watched these people all her life and learned to imitate their dress, style, and manners. Anyone who meets her would never guess she grew up on the Lower East Side of parents who spoke only Yiddish. But she loves going back there.

Frieda looks nervously at her watch. She's late, not much, but just enough. She rises from the subway and glances across the street at the familiar *Jewish Daily Forward* building. She sniffs the air. Unmistakable. The Garden bakes fresh challah bread every Friday. She'll take a loaf home if there are any left. She turns the corner with the Cafeteria sign in rounded metal letters, and pushes the revolving door. Abe is already at a table, poking a finger at his watch and glowering beneath his bushy black brows.

"You're ten minutes late!" he shouts. "Why is it you can never be on time? Do you do it deliberately? I'm holding a table at their busiest hour. You don't give yourself enough time to get anywhere. You're always thinking about something else. I told you it was hard for me to get away from the bakery floor and then you make me wait!"

His voice cuts through the clank of dishes and silverware, and the ebullient chatter at the red Formica tables. The folks intent on their platters of lox and cream cheese and their mushroom and barley soups look over at them.

"Please, Abe." She tugs at his sleeve, but he jerks his hand away. "Please. I'm really sorry." She nods in the direction of the diners nearby.

"All right. All right." His voice softens. She has that effect on him. She knows it and she uses it.

"Did you order?" she asks.

"Of course, I ordered. And I know you like the kasha varnishkas. So… you're looking very pretty today. I like the hat." His anger is a summer storm. Here. Gone. He scorches with lightning, then soothes like gentle rain. Not an easy man, her mama says. Yet generous, Mama admits. Exciting too, but Frieda is not telling that to Mama.

The counterman calls Abe's number and he snatches the ticket from the table and dashes to pick up their tray, for her the bow-ties beaded with kasha, for him, the smoked whitefish with lettuce and tomatoes and a thick slice of black bread. Abe's white baker's coat flaps at his ankles as he strides towards her. When he sits down, he tucks the napkin into the collar of the starched white shirt he always wears with a striped tie under the coat. Her husband has large hands, long fingers and, despite his gruff exterior, fine table manners he learned from those cultured Latvian Jews who died before she could meet them.

"It's all about knowing the neighborhood and satisfying the customer," Abe is saying. "It's no accident everyone comes to The Garden, I always tell Charlie."

Charlie Metzger is moving towards their table, an expansive host with his square jaw, thick white head of hair, and warm smile.

"Abe! Hello, Frieda," he says. "I thought I saw you come in. it's been a while. An occasion, the two of you together?"

"Frieda's playing at the settlement house today, so we thought, why not eat at The Garden?"

"It's always so delicious," Frieda wipes a grain from the corner of mouth. She looks up into Metzger's gray-green eyes, "and somehow you manage to make everyone feel at home."

"Well, I hope Abe will stick around for some pinochle. The usual. After the lunch crowd."

"Not today. I have to get back. I got such trouble with the unions, you won't believe," Abe says.

"I know. I know. Same here." Metzger says, lowering his voice.

"The price of staying in business." Abe crosses one palm with two fingers of his other hand. Someone always needs to be paid off.

"And what about the shortages? How you managing? Butter, flour, sugar. I'm a dairy restaurant. I go from day to day. And you? With a bakery?"

"Like you say, it's not easy. You can't make rolls and cakes from air and water. "

"But we find a way, don't we? We'll miss you at pinochle, Abe. Nice to see you Frieda. You're looking lovely. You should come down more often."

Charlie squeezes Abe's upper arm before moving on and settling in at a table against the wall beside four men with fedora hats, all talking at once.

"They're writers from *The Jewish Daily Forward*." Abe nods towards the table. "He doesn't care that they're socialists. They're his buddies. I don't know how Charlie does it. He also knows every businessman in the neighborhood. The man makes connections. And the patience! He chews out the counterman or the cashier when they're slow and forget things, but the customers? Never. I couldn't do it in a million years. Butter—even in a shortage—wouldn't melt in his mouth."

"You do have wonderful qualities, Abe, but patience isn't one of them."

"So… how's our Alice today?"

"I'm worried about her with the move and all."

Alice comes home alone, slams her bedroom door, and, although she has always been a chatterbox, volunteers nothing when Frieda asks about her day. Maybe it was a mistake to send her to private school when they moved from Brooklyn. Maybe ten is a bad age to make such a change. Girls can be very mean at that age.

"Yesterday, she argued with me about what she should wear. She said the other girls say she dresses funny. Actually, what they said, according to Alice, was 'Your mother dresses you funny.' Isn't that awful. Abe? I don't know what kids that age wear in fancy private schools in Manhattan. She says the girls collect cashmere sweaters. They cost a fortune. *I* don't even own one. It seems like an indulgence for a child. They all have to have the latest this, the latest that. I hear the mothers talking. If you haven't gone to London or Paris on your vacation and stayed at the Ritz, you might as well have stayed home. Forget Florida. Only greenhorns go to Florida."

"What do you want me to do, Frieda? I mean about Alice. Should I talk to that woman, what do they call her— the head mistress? I'll make an appointment next week."

For her husband like a lot of the men she knows, conversation is all about getting the job *done,* not finding out what the job *is.*

"Just listen to me. I'm wondering whether we should take Alice out at the end of the semester. Maybe send her to the public school where the children aren't rich and privileged."

"But didn't you say this is a better education? Isn't that why we sent her there in the first place? Alice is so smart and you didn't want her to be bored. She'll work it out. If it takes a cashmere sweater or two, buy them. And while you're at it, get one for yourself."

"That's not the point."

"Gotta go, dear. Now the unions, that's a *real* problem." He brushes her lips with his. "I'll try to get home early. And don't worry so much, Alice has a good head on her shoulders."

"Like her father?"

"If you say so."

"I know, I know. You came to America at seventeen without a word of English."

"But it's true. I did." He kisses her again.

Mr. Velt, the program director for the settlement house, holds open the heavy blue door. He wears a black suit, purpled with age, a bright red bowtie, and he leans on a pearl-handled cane.

"Ah, Mrs. Gold. So good to see you. We are eager and waiting as you can tell."

"My pleasure, Mr. Velt. Hello everyone," Frieda calls out with forced gaiety. Her own life is too good. She moves to the Steinway and puts her music on the rack, then turns towards the gathering. The room is gray and shabby like the audience, all in their seventies and eighties, some with canes and walkers, sitting in quiet rows on metal folding chairs, looking out at her through cloudy eyes. A few smile and say, "Hello, Mrs. Gold."

She's always struck by the silence. It's as though they forgot how to talk to one another and what to talk about. During the reception of cookies and tea that follows each of her performances, she tries to draw them out with questions. One shapeless, colorless woman had been a nurse, another a concert singer. A dried stick of a man told her about the death of his mother in the Triangle Factory fire.

"She didn't come home. She never came home again." Frieda held his hand and he cried like a child. Another managed a dramatic account of the affair between the beautiful actress Evelyn Nesbitt and the architect Stanford White, shot dead by the jealous husband, Harry Kay Thaw. And don't get him started on the kidnapping of the Lindbergh baby! Yesterday's news made vivid and immediate. At the same time, they all seem distanced from what is happening right now, the war raging in Europe, the war that's killing the Jews. Better a tragic fire in a factory, a sex scandal, a kidnapped goyish baby.

But on a day when Alice had an after-school project, Frieda lingered with Mr. Velt and a few others, all old Lefties it turned out, to listen to the disturbing news from the front. At six o'clock, they gathered around the large Bakelite radio.

"Schrechlicht. It's schrechlicht," said one of the men, using the Yiddish word for terrible.

"And that's the good news," another countered, "God knows what they're not telling us."

The applause is loud and long.

"They'd give you a standing ovation if they could stand," whispers Mr. Velt. Frieda asks whether there are

129

any requests for next week. Although she no longer teaches piano, she still practices three hours a day and has a large repertoire.

"Some Bach please, Mrs. Gold. We require transcendence. The Italian Concerto? You know, maybe, the Italian Concerto?"

"Not well, but I'll learn it. Maybe not next time but the time after."

"It is, I admit, a difficult piece of music. Bach was no sissy."

She looks at the man. "I don't think we've met." She holds out her hand and he grasps it firmly.

"Irving Mursky. I know your mother, Mrs. Sarah Feldman, right? From the Workman's Circle."

"That's Mama."

"Your mother is quite a force, Mrs. Gold."

"She is that. Mama does good work in the world whether the world wants it or not." She's sorry the minute it's out of her mouth. "Of course, I admire my mother. She's amazing."

"And I understand you play here every week. Our commitments define us."

Oh, she hopes as she leaves, don't let this place gray you down, Mr. Mursky. She will remember: "We require transcendence," "Bach was no sissy," "Our commitments define us." She collects phrases like others do jewels. For her, they *are* jewels to set in the stories she tells. But she will need to work hard on the Italian Concerto if she's going to play it up to tempo. She'll have to talk to Eugenie, her Russian piano teacher. "Keep learning or die," is Frieda's motto.

She won't be staying for the reception this afternoon, she tells Mr. Velt.

"Not today. I need to get home." But Mr. Velt won't let her leave so easily.

"I'm thinking of changing my name officially to Welt," he says. "Our people have a hard time with V's. They call me Mr. Welt anyway, so I might as well spell it with a W. What do you think?'

"Are you serious?" She has her hand on the doorknob. "Velt" means *world* in Yiddish and "Welt" means nothing important.

"The problem is," Mr. Velt continues, "our people also have a hard time with W's. If I change my name to Welt,

131

they'll call me Mr. Velt. Try getting any of them to say Van Wyck Expressway. It's a regular tongue twister around here."

"You're joking about the name change, right?"

"Of course, I'm joking. I'm always joking. Who doesn't need a laugh these days?"

"Goodbye, Mr. Velt-Welt. See you next week." Frieda shakes his hand and is out the door. She wants to be in the apartment the moment Alice comes home at four. Alice scolded her once when Frieda told a neighbor she always got back in time to see Alice after school.

"No, you don't."

"Ok, sometimes I'm fifteen minutes late. But I'm always there."

"It's the first fifteen minutes that counts," Alice said, folding her arms across her chest in that mock grown-up way she has. Frieda doesn't like Alice contradicting her in public, but what she said makes sense. After the first fifteen minutes of telling her mother what is exciting or troubling or whatever about her day, the child goes off to read or at least when they lived in Brooklyn, pick up the phone to call the friend she just said goodbye to on the corner.

132

Frieda rushes through Katz's Delicatessen on Houston Street and orders sliced pastrami, a loaf of seeded rye, sour kraut, potato salad, and pickles. The counterman fishes the sour pickles out of a barrel with a wooden ladle. Lunch for Saturday. She inhales the store, the smells of the Lower East Side, salty, tangy, musty. She and her girlfriends always stopped at a deli for a sour pickle on their way home from school. She longs to reach into the brown paper bag and pull one out right now. But no well-bred lady eats a pickle on the street or on the subway.

"What do you want to do tomorrow, Alice?" Frieda asks soon after Alice unlocks the front door.

"A movie? I bought us pastrami for lunch with potato salad, sour kraut, and pickles. "

"Too much homework," Alice grunts, goes into her room and slams the door. So much for the first fifteen minutes. Although it is already the end of November, Alice has yet to bring a friend home from school. Frieda is not as sure as her husband that Alice can manage this change without help.

After she scours the apartment and the sun shines across the dining table without lighting a single mote of dust, Frieda brings the antique lamp to the Polish repair shop for rewiring, and the blue glass beads to that Viennese refugee for restringing. She heads uptown to 88th and Eugenie's studio in one of the wind tunnels between Broadway and Riverside Drive. She's blown up the steps of the brownstone stoop, the wind firmly at her back. Eugenie's studio is on the first floor with a bay window overlooking the street, a large bed smothered in colorful pillows, an oriental rug, and a baby grand that fills the other half of the room. When you push open the tall carved doors, you can't help but imagine the parlor as it once was when the house was an elegant single-family home.

She's early. A young man is still taking his lesson, bent in boyish awkwardness over the keyboard. He looks about fifteen. Frieda settles quietly into the window seat and listens to a Mendelsohn Love Song. The young man secures every note and executes each phrase with perfection to the ticking metronome on the music rack. Eugenie doesn't take just anyone and this boy is talented. But Eugenie, a big woman wearing a loose peasant blouse and multiple necklaces, keeps frowning and shaking her head. This Eddie—Frieda remembers his name is Eddie Sloane,

134

she met him at the last student recital—is not playing Mendelsohn as she would like. He finishes. Eugenie sighs.

"Ehdgie," Eugenie begins. "Dis is Luf song. You are s'posed to play eet like you are saying, 'I Luf You. I Luf you. I Luf You.' You know how you play eet?"

"No, Miss Sledon." The boy looks at her and his eyes dart down to the brass pedals at his feet.

"You play eet like you are saying," and here Eugenie raises her voice like a street vendor, "'I sell fresh feesh! I sell fresh feesh!'"

"But I thought…I mean I practiced…"

"Of course. You have all the notes. Now, you must work on the feeling."

Eddie Sloane is out the door in a minute. Tonight, Abe will have a laugh over that one. Through the years, Frieda has perfected Eugenie's Russian accent.

"So, my dahlink Frieda." Big hug. "What can you do? These young people. No emotion. No passion. It's just notes, notes, notes to them. All the same. Up and down the keyboard. Like machines they play. Your Alice, she's different. She is all emotion and no notes. The child should practice. She could learn from my Ehdgie."

135

"I'm worried about Alice, Eugenie." She tells the piano teacher why.

"You must go to that school immediately. The child is sohffering. Alice, she is not talking? Alice not talking? I can't eeemagine it. I tell you, she's sohffering. If you want sohffering, stay in Russia. You must speak to those people at the school. Put a stop to this. End of discussion. So, what do you want to play today?"

Frieda tells her about the Italian Concerto.

"Good. Bach then. It's too much Chopin. I tell you last time. You will do Italian beeeautifully." She opens the music on the rack. "Start here. Very slowly. And one. And two."

The tuition bill for the spring semester is on the top of the pile. It's the middle of December and Alice has been coming home in tears almost every day. She's finally talking. And it's not good.

"They all hate me, Mom."

"That's impossible. You've always made friends easily. You're a very likable girl."

"That's what *you* think. But I left all my friends in Brooklyn."

"What do they do? These children at your school."

"They pick on me. They make fun of me. They make me sit alone at lunch. They laugh at my shoes and my hair and the way I throw a baseball in the park. Who cares about throwing a stupid baseball? The boys like Peter and Hugh are nice, but the girls are just mean. When I get an A, they say I'm a goody goody, a teacher's pet."

"They're just jealous."

"I tried to be nice to them like you said, but it doesn't work. Don't send me back after the holiday. Please, Mom. I don't want to go back. They're persecuting me...like the Nazis are persecuting Jews only all of us are Jewish so it's not about an ideology."

"Don't say that, dear. Don't trivialize the Nazi persecutions. This is different. This is just kids being mean. But I'm impressed you used the word *ideology*. You see you *are* getting a good education in spite of it all. I knew it. You didn't know that word last year. You certainly couldn't have used it correctly in a sentence."

"Who cares? You can look it up in Webster's. But I hate it there. I hate it all. They talk about morality in discussion blah, blah, blah, and then they let these kids be mean and no one does anything about it."

Frieda sees the head mistress the next morning. Miss Whedon is a fortyish woman with a brown pageboy haircut, and she wears a stylish, but conservative blue dress with a square neckline and shirring at the shoulders. She has a slight British accent, no doubt cultivated to make her seem…well, British…and heir to that fine educational tradition. The parents love Miss Whedon.

Frieda settles into the chair opposite and stares at a large glass paperweight that entraps a once-live purple violet. There isn't a piece of paper on the desk. Frieda wants to inform this ice queen that her daughter, Alice, is very unhappy at her precious school. No point minimizing it. The girls are mean to her and exclude her. Haven't her teachers noticed?

"I asked and yes, they have. They say Alice is an excellent student."

"Of course. I know that. But can't something be done? Can't you hold a meeting and talk about what it means to pick on another child? Couldn't this be an opportunity for a lesson in empathy?"

"Of course, we can have a meeting. But it won't do any good. Children this age are just like that. And your Alice is quite different from the other girls. The way she dresses and speaks, and the way she behaves."

"She *is* different. She's completely original. She doesn't care about clothes or baseball. She has a rich inner life."

"Well, if she's to get along here, she will have to become more like the other children. It's really quite simple."

"Not for us, Mrs. Whedon. It's not simple at all." Frieda says, putting on her camel's hair coat and wrapping the belt around her waist.

"I don't want Alice to become like the other children. My husband and I have decided not to send her back here next semester. I like her just the way she is."

Frieda goes down the steps of the school, still enjoying the ill-concealed surprise on Mrs. Wheden's generally impassive face. She walks towards the bus stop, reviewing the scene in the office, the sterile desk, the fake English headmistress, the heavy paperweight without purpose. She breathes the fresh winter air. When she gets off the bus, the sky is white with the possibility of snow and a block from her building, the flakes begin to fall gently into a stillness she embraces as her own. The young doorman opens the glass door to the lobby.

"Good day, Mrs. Gold," he says. "It looks like we're in for some snow."

"Yes, Thomas. Lovely, isn't it? But it's always nice to be home."

THE IMPRESSIONIST

She's a good-looking woman, no question about it. Brown hair she dyed blonde when she got into her thirties, even features, dazzling smile. Lively. Phil met Bertha at a party and since he doesn't enjoy small talk, it was a relief to find someone who could manage both sides of the conversation. People tell him he looks like Humphrey Bogart, and like Bogart, he can make a few words go a long way. Sometimes a silent man is considered profound. And the truth is Phil does think a lot. And plan. And plot.

The real problem was Bertha's family.

"You marry the family," his mother used to say. "Always pay attention to what they're like because you're going to spend the rest of your life with them." And boy, was she ever right. Phil married into the Feldman family, married the matriarch Sarah Feldman's youngest and prettiest daughter. And then, even though he was the foreman of a factory and a good manager, he lost his job. The Depression didn't discriminate. Experienced; beginners; lazy; hard workers. Everyone was out of work.

You couldn't blame yourself. On the other hand, even people who don't feel guilty need food and housing.

"I can't believe it," Bertha said. "And at the worst time." Harvey was six months old.

She didn't have much tact, that woman. But she kissed him and wound her arms around his neck. Then she kissed his neck. The thing was Bertha always had her hands all over him. He felt like saying "down, dog" or "keep your hands to yourself" like kids do in school. It wasn't only when they were alone; she was also all over him when they were out, like she needed to plant a flag on her territory.

They lived in the same building in Brooklyn as Bertha's older sister Frieda and her husband Abe. He actually liked Frieda. She was not like a lot of the Feldmans', always expressing themselves, always offering an unsolicited opinion. Frieda was a class act; a pianist, quiet, cultured, refined. She made each book she was reading sound like something he would want to read if he ever had the time to read. She recommended an Impressionist show at the Metropolitan Museum and he went alone. He didn't want Bertha to come and gab the whole time about how maybe they could go to those places in the paintings. He walked from gallery to gallery, transported into that shimmery world where women held parasols and boats glided down rivers and churches glowed in the sunshine. He thanked Frieda and while she often suggested other shows, he never went again. It was enough for him.

One summer, he and Bertha joined Frieda and Abe at the seashore with their children, and Abe, his brother-in-law, insisted on picking up all the dinner checks. The guy *was* generous. Came to this country without a penny and built a successful commercial bakery downtown. Of course, he'd heard *that* story more than once.

But after Phil lost his job, things got pretty tense. When Harvey napped, Bertha spent lots of time going upstairs to visit Frieda, play Mah Jong, and complain about him—no gumption, no guts. Not true. He was really trying to get work. He just didn't want to talk about it.

One afternoon, when he was taking a break from pounding the pavement, Bertha came back and threw her arms around him.

"We figured it out, Frieda and me," she said.

"So?"

"Frieda is going to get Abe to give you a job at the bakery."

"It's not that I haven't thought about that, Bertha. It's logical, given my experience. But if the man really wanted me, he would have asked me himself."

"Well, you're right about that, Phil."

"See? I'm not working for someone who doesn't want me. And with Abe it's always 'my way or the highway.' He's that kind of guy. So, tell Frieda to forget it."

"But you have skills, Phil. You know how to run a factory. And like I said to Frieda. Phil is family. It's not like Abe would be trusting his place to a stranger. But it turns out, that's actually the problem, you being family."

"Really? How come?"

"Frieda told me Abe doesn't think it's a good idea to employ relatives on principle. He says business and family don't mix. She told me Uncle Sidney was working for Abe until Abe found out Sidney was selling rolls and cakes off the loading platform like a private business. He had his own customers, would you believe it?"

"I'm not surprised about Sidney, but I'd never do anything that stupid," Phil says. "Of course, you'd eventually be found out."

Only a week later, the doorbell rang and it was Abe stopping by after work. The conversation was brief. Abe said he thought he could use Phil in the bakery and asked if he was interested. He needed an assistant manager, someone on the bakery floor. And he even admitted that Phil had good and appropriate experience. Actually, Phil felt he was over-qualified for the position, but at that point he and Bertha had used up their savings and couldn't pay the rent. So, he went to work for his brother-in-law.

The United States was at war and it was hard to get basic supplies for the bakery: butter, flour, sugar. But Phil knew who you had to see and whose palm you had to grease. And he found new suppliers who were willing to give him a cut to get the business. Like everyone said, Phil Kaminer was a smooth customer. That he was a quiet man who, like they said, kept his own counsel, certainly didn't hurt. He made friends with the president of the union local and struck deals that were good for both of them. Abe was building a new factory in Bayonne and busy with plans, so he began leaving some of the day to day operations to Phil. Somehow, though, the new job didn't bring Phil and Bertha any closer to Abe and Frieda. Quite the opposite. Employees and bosses don't generally socialize. Too much private information neither wants to share. It's also true Abe moved the family out of Brooklyn and to a fancy apartment on Central Park West. He was clearly making a lot of money. And Bertha became demanding. She wanted a mink coat like her sister's, an antique gold watch like Frieda's, the latest purse or pumps, again, of course, like Frieda's. But unlike Frieda, Bertha had bad taste. Even he could see that. And everything she bought for the house was garish and gaudy. Mirrors with heavy carving. Glitzy chandeliers. The place looked like a whorehouse. And he should know.

"You don't seem to understand, Phil. I want to move up in the world," Bertha said. "I want the very best. We deserve it. You're working so hard. You don't even get home in time to tuck Harvey into bed." She wriggled onto his lap and gave him a French kiss. She favored heavy perfumes like Gardenia. He thought he'd throw up.

Truth was he didn't come straight home after work. He and the bakery's top salesman, Harry London, who changed his name from Landtsman, usually stopped off for a drink at a place they liked near the East River. In the warm weather, they set up tables outdoors close to the water. Even with the traffic, you could hear waves lapping at the dock and tugboats tooting in the dusk. The boats cut through their own reflections and made ripples like in an Impressionist painting. Sometimes Harry's pretty kid sister, Lily, came along with them. Harry had gotten Lily part-time work operating the switchboard at the bakery, taking and transferring phone calls. Lily kept telling Phil he was a dead ringer for Humphrey Bogart.

Phil asked Abe for a raise. He'd been there long enough. The war was over and everyone was feeling flush. Abe had no problem with that. He raised Phil's salary by twenty-five percent and changed his title from Assistant Manager to Manager. Phil had been functioning as Manager for at least two years, so it was nice Abe finally did something about it.

"Buy something pretty for Bertha," Abe said. "Just between you and me, I think she's feeling neglected. You know how women are. Go down to the Jewelry Exchange. Get her a gold brooch. Better yet, a watch. And here why don't you take the family out for a good dinner to celebrate." Abe handed him a crisp fifty-dollar bill. His brother-in-law always had a roll of newly-minted bills in his pocket. Just to make sure you knew how successful he was. Like the new Buick every year with the white wall tires.

Bertha got even more affectionate, if that was possible, when she heard about the raise. Phil never went down to the Jewelry Exchange and he pocketed the fifty bucks and got himself a couple of silk ties. Bertha bought herself a gold necklace and told everyone her husband bought it for her.

Something else changed with the raise. It started with Abe's unexpected visits to the factory floor, his finding a machine that hadn't been cleaned, a worker smoking too close to the conveyer belt, an order that, according to his standards, hadn't been packed right.

"What the hell you doing, Phil?" he would shout.

"Are you in charge here or not?!" And when Phil made any suggestions for improvement in the line, Abe would shoot it down.

"You got big ideas? Keep them to yourself. I'm the one with the ideas. You're the one who makes sure they're carried out. Got it?!"

The money was good, but Abe made Phil feel bad. And when he watched his wife competing with her older sister in clothes, in decorating, in lavish entertaining, he saw Frieda made Bertha feel bad too. He didn't care for Bertha much anymore—in fact, he had already started fooling around with London's sister Lily—but he wasn't going to have Abe and Frieda put his wife down.

He began talking to London about how they could go out on their own. Start a competing bakery. Same clientele. He knew the formulas for the most successful products— the cinnamon rolls, the buns, the crumb cakes, the rye, the pumpernickel—and London knew all the top customers. They met every night after work to talk about it. Abe was such a straight shooter himself, he wasn't even suspicious.

Phil Kaminer and Harry London handed in their notices and opened up for business. That became one of the Feldman family scandals, as Phil's son Harvey would say: "one of the top hits of 1947." Bertha was supportive, of course. She felt bad about Frieda, because she loved her sister, but like they say, she stood by her man. And she admired his guts. She even got pregnant although they didn't have sex very much anymore and Harvey was already eight years old.

It was probably a big blow to Abe's business—top salesman gone, big customers lured away. That was fine with Phil. But most significant for the Feldman family, the two couples were no longer on speaking terms. Frieda called him once and in soft measured tones.

"I don't know how you could do this, Phil." She said. "Abe has been so good to you. He gave you work at the height of the Depression. He paid you well. And this? This betrayal. I'm afraid Abe and I can't see you and Bertha and Harvey anymore. It's over. You've managed to destroy our family." She didn't wait to hear what he had to say. She hung up.

Phil still liked and respected Frieda, but he was happy to be free of the Feldmans. He and Bertha hardly ever went to family meetings. The problem was keeping a wife and two sons and having a mistress was expensive and so, even though the new bakery was doing well, he was always strapped for cash. When it was time for his son Harvey to have his Bar Mitzvah, he told Bertha she'd have to scale back on the party. He added he had loaned Abe ten thousand dollars a few years ago and the bastard never paid it back. And, if there was any chance of reconciliation between the sisters and brothers-in-law, this lie about the ten-thousand-dollar loan, even though necessary, ensured it wouldn't happen.

Frieda spoke to him only once again, when they saw each other at the hospital. His mother-in-law, the indestructible Sarah Feldman, was very sick. Abe paid the bills for nurses around the clock, and Bertha, Frieda, and their older sister Mildred wept together at their mother's bedside. Phil spent most of the time in the waiting room, reading the paper and napping or going to the phone booth in the hall to call Lily. Frieda saw him out there.

"How do you sleep nights, Phil? How?" She asked, then turned on her heel and went back down the hospital hallway towards her mother.

Phil actually slept very well, thank you, and sometimes mid-afternoons as well. Mostly with Lily. He was obsessed with her. He had found not only a successful business, maybe never as successful as Abe's but not bad, but he also found the love of his life. He stayed married to Bertha—at least the Feldmans didn't have to deal with the scandal of divorce—but he stole every moment he could to be with Lily, even after she married her high school boyfriend and had a couple of kids.

Theirs was a grand passion, an addiction, something only the French understand. One year he even took Lily to Paris, a business trip, a write-off, to make a study of baguettes, maybe croissants too. And when they drove down to the south of France, he finally found the landscape that inspired the Impressionist paintings he had seen so many years ago at the Metropolitan Museum, the rolling green hills, the dappled sunlight, and the glistening river. He and Lily spread a blanket on the grass and picnicked on bread, cheese, and wine. He pulled her close to him and she stroked his dark hair, now speckled with gray. Phil gazed at the dappled water, black with short brush strokes like a

Monet painting, and enjoyed the gentle pressure of Lily's small breasts against his chest.

WITNESS TO HISTORY

I used to lock myself in the bathroom stall and cry when the girls picked on me. My cousin Hanna says they teased me because I was the only new girl in the sixth grade. But some of them just like being mean. Hanna says there are people all over the world who enjoy making other people suffer. Like Hitler and Goering and Goebbels. I wrote a story and made the meanest girl—that Nancy Weiss—a bad character. When the teacher read my story aloud in class, Nancy knew I was talking about her. So did everyone else. She turned bright red, and started shifting around in her seat. She thinks she's special because she has blond curls you just want to dip in the inkwell. She's lucky I don't sit behind her. When she heard my story, she asked to be excused. She went to the bathroom and didn't come back for a long time.

"Good for you," Hanna said when I told her. Hanna is twenty-one. My dad brought her here from Latvia right before the war. After that, you couldn't get out.

"Writing is a powerful weapon," Hanna says. "Look at I.F. Stone. Or even Edgar Mowrer."

"Sure," I say. They must be important writers.

Then Hanna says, "But you have to be accurate if you want to be a witness to history."

Witness to history, sounds good, doesn't it? That's what I'm going to be.

Now I'm eleven, I can go to Hanna's apartment by myself. It's easy to get anywhere on the bus. I like to buy a hot dog from the Sabrett man on the corner who always calls out "Hotta Dogga." He doesn't just have an accent like Lydia from Poland who says "stop spleshink" when anyone gets close to her in the pool. The hot dog man doesn't speak any English at all. He only knows "Hotta Dogga." I can tell because I tried talking to him and he didn't understand a word. He just smiled and pulled the pale pink hot dog out of the cloudy water, smeared it with mustard and handed it to me in a paper napkin. It's better to know English to get along in this country. Dad told me how hard it was for him. It was easier for Hanna because she went to a good school in Riga and was *fluent* when she came. Maybe the hot dog man will let me teach him some

English. I could do it like an after-school activity, like a kind of social service. I could buy a second hot dog, so he'd know I also want to help his business.

The bus belches to the corner with a smelly blast. I get a seat near a window. The mustard is drippy, but I catch it with the napkin before it gets to my plaid skirt. I love Hanna's new place, a studio with a pull-out sofa, a two-burner stove, board and brick shelves stacked with books, an Underwood typewriter, and a desk with cubbyholes. I can read all afternoon there without Mom telling me to do my homework or clean out my closet. I always do my homework and my closet is full of stuff I need. Get used to it, Mom. Hanna and I listen to classical music, popular singers, or the news.

"Just hear this, Alice," Hanna says as soon as I come in. She's talking loud and fast like she does when she's upset.

"Front page of your dad's favorite paper. It's a dispatch from Switzerland. The Nazis are boasting to the entire world about what they're doing. They want to create what they call 'a Jewish State behind barbed wire… severed from any connection with the world, left to live and deal with each other.' The article quotes this Rosenberg, head of the Department of Jewish Questions. Rosenberg is in charge of the German occupied territories of the East."

"That's means Latvia, doesn't it? Where our family is? Your dad and Uncle Sol and Aunt Lotte?"

"Of course."

I want to go back to my book. I'm reading *Jean Christophe*. It's a love story and way ahead of my grade level. I know I should hear more about what's happening, so I can become political like Hanna, but sometimes it's too awful and I just want to be a kid and not have to think about it. But Hanna won't let me. My dad says she's *relentless*.

She goes on reading aloud:

"'Jews must be cast off and guarded by sentries. Jews must work inside their ghettos.' This Rosenberg wants to 'prevent the spread of the Jewish influence to other parts of the world. The projected Nazi code will realize the ultimate aim of the anti-Jewish policy, namely ridding Europe of the last Jew.'" Hanna throws the paper down on the table.

"There it is," she says. "Front page news. In the establishment Bible—*The New York Times*. Not what your father calls one of my socialist rags. And you know what's really bad, Alice? The most powerful American Jews are too afraid of the anti-Semites to speak up. They think there will be backlash. Ridiculous. I've heard it all my life. I hate it. If they speak up—some are really close to Roosevelt—we could save people even now."

"And what will they do? It says they're going to rid Europe of the last Jew. How will they do that?"

I ask Hanna if I can cut the article out, so I can bring it to school. I have to go home before it gets dark.

I read the article again on the bus going back. Everyone believes *The New York Times*, even if Hanna says it doesn't always tell the whole story. But here it is. The Nazis are bragging. They're saying 'look at what we're doing. We're proud of ourselves. And we know you will be too.'

Why do they think everyone would want to 'prevent the spread of Jewish influence'? My mom and Bubbe, *her* mom, say Jews are a *good* influence, because part of the Jewish tradition is to help others and make the world a better place. But maybe everyone else doesn't know this about us. The Nazis wouldn't brag if they didn't think people would agree with them, right?

The next morning, I stop on the corner of Broadway and 72ⁿᵈ Street. My best friend Ruth Saltzman comes up the block from where she lives above her father's jewelry store. Ruth and her family came to New York five years ago. They all have heavy accents. Mom says if you come here before you're eleven, you will lose your accent, so Ruth will. Mom also says she will only buy watches from Mr. Saltzman. She supports Jewish refugees whenever she can. Mostly that means buying things from them or bringing them things to fix.

"There's a scary article in the *Times*," I tell Ruth when we start walking uptown towards school. I tell her what it says. "I cut it out for Current Events. I'm going to ask Mrs. Bloch to talk about it. Everyone is saying we had to go to war. Everyone is following the battles. But we have to save Jewish people over there and no one wants to talk about it."

"My aunt and uncle are in Poland. In Warsaw."

"Where the ghetto is. That's what this Rosenberg calls, 'the Jewish State behind barbed wire' like he's making fun of a Jewish State in Palestine. My Uncle Sol is in Latvia.

He came to see us, but he went back. And my father won't talk about anything with me."

"My mom and dad too. They want to protect me."

"But no one is protecting Jewish children in Europe. Some people are just as happy to let it happen. To stop what they call 'the spread of Jewish influence.' I thought Jews were a good influence, didn't you?"

"He went back, your uncle?" Ruth asks.

I don't like what Mrs. Bloch says so I take notes. That's what you do if you want to be a witness to history.

"It's good that you follow what's happening in the world, Alice."

"It's not hard. This plan to eliminate the Jews was on the front page of the *Times*."

"You have relatives over there, right?"

"But this is about much more than my Uncle Sol and Aunt Lotte."

"Well I know, dear, but I'm afraid your article isn't appropriate to discuss in class. It would upset the children."

"But Mrs. Bloch, we've been studying the war. We have a map with pins and everything. This is about Hitler's plan for the Jews."

"It will be too hard for the children to understand."

"It's pretty simple. Hitler wants to get rid of every single Jew."

"Don't say that, Alice."

"I'm not saying it; this Rosenberg is saying it. And Hitler put him in charge."

"Well, maybe. But I'm not having this discussed in class. I'm sorry, dear, I know this means a lot to you."

"Not just to *me,* Mrs. Bloch. Aren't you Jewish too?"

Mrs. Bloch gets very busy rearranging the Delaney cards in their folder. Each card has the name of a student and helps teachers keep track of who they are and where they sit. Mr. Delaney must have invented the system. That's how you get your name on things.

After the bell rings, we all race down the steps and into the school yard. It's one of those warm February days when everything seems to be thawing and the picnic table near the wire fence where we hang out is drippy. I run into the girls' room and get a bunch of paper towels and we wipe it off. Then I pull out the article. Wow, my friends say. They can't believe it. We're Americans and we're not used to what Ruth calls 'a public announcement of persecution.'

161

My friends at P.S. 84 are pretty much all Jewish, except Patrick, and the article upsets them like Mrs. Bloch said, but in a good way.

Susan pulls out a Hershey bar from her schoolbag and breaks off enough pieces to hand around. She thinks we should hold a meeting after school next week, get permission to use the auditorium and find a speaker. Hanna could get us someone. Ruth puts a rubber band around her blond hair and says that will make us feel good like we're doing something, but information isn't enough. She thinks we should write letters to President Roosevelt. But Barbara, who's turned into a know-it-all this past year, says that the President never reads those letters. Some secretary tosses them into a wastebasket and sends you back a form letter. Patrick says Barbara's right. He's taller than any of us and always gets attention.

"Besides, we're not old enough to vote," Patrick says. "Why would the President care what we think?" His Dad is with the Democrats. Then the Good Humor truck lets us know it's here by playing its little song and everyone forgets that we were talking about something really serious and we go for ice cream. I have a chocolate pop. I like to make it last, but you can't tell until you're finished whether you got a lucky stick. It's printed 'Lucky Stick' in small brown letters. That means they give you a free extra ice cream. Once, it even happened to me.

"We have to get some grown-ups on our side," I say when we go back to the picnic table. "Like our principal, Miss Walinski. She's Jewish and maybe not like Mrs. Bloch-head. That's how come she got to be a principal."

"The teachers should be teaching about this," Ruth says. "Not just in social studies. I have an aunt and uncle in Poland."

"My grandma is in Lithuania, but she can't write to us anymore."

"We haven't heard from my Uncle Sol in over a year," I say.

"I have an idea," Josh says. He's always so quiet you forget him. But he stores up stuff like a squirrel. He looks like one too, small and frisky with buckteeth.

"Let's throw a picket line around the school," Josh says. "They should be teaching us this stuff about Hitler and what he wants to do to Jewish people. My dad is with the garment workers and they always picket when they want to get the bosses to do something. It works, too."

"Well the teachers are our bosses," Barbara says. "They act like bosses anyway." She should know. She's pretty bossy herself.

Of course, I should have thought of a picket line. Hanna Gottlieb, my own cousin, is a big shot in her union.

The next day the six of us meet in Barbara's finished basement. We girls decide Josh and Patrick are OK. They never chase you around the yard for no reason, pull your braids, and make fun of the way you throw a ball. They act almost as grown-up and sensible as girls. "Besides," Ruth points out "Picketing was Josh's idea."

We collect those shirt cardboards from our dads' drawers, the kind the cleaners put inside starched shirts. They're gray, but just the right size for signs. We've got little bottles of colored ink. Hanna has taken me to a couple of rallies and hand-lettered signs are the best. But what should they say? We argue. Has to be short and catchy, I tell them. "Three slogans are plenty."

Patrick is leaning over the ping pong table and Barbara tells him he's going to break it. "You serious?" Patrick says. "It looks pretty strong to me."

"You want to stay?" Barbara says.

We girls are going to dress in black—like we're in mourning—black t-shirts and black leotards from dance class. Also, our black Capezio ballet slippers. We tell Patrick and Josh to do black shirts and pants. Patrick says he's going to wear his black belt and the brass buckle with the skull and crossbones. We're writing our signs in black ink, with red ink spilling down from the letters like blood. We have to throw out a few because they get messy, but we have enough good ones.

We're going to march back and forth in front of the steps before the bell rings at 8:30. We're pretty sure no one in our school will cross a picket line. We'll wave our signs and chant together: "No Time To Lose/Save the Jews" and "Don't Refuse/Teach War On Jews" and "Stop Hitler's War/At P.S. 84". I don't tell my mother because she'll tell my father and he will be angry. He'll blame Hanna. He hates her politics. I don't tell Hanna because she has an opinion on everything and I want to do this myself.

What can I say? Someone ratted us out. When we get to school, the school guards are waiting for us. They let us march for maybe five minutes. Then they run at us, take our signs, and make us go inside. One grabs my arm so hard it stays black and blue for a week. I yell "Free speech. What happened to free speech?" Susan's father works for NBC and he's there too. One of his guys interviews me and Josh after school. On the radio that night, they talk about the demonstration at P.S. 84. Which of course my dad hears. And now he's sure his socialist niece Hanna got us to picket. He won't listen when I tell him it was my idea. He sends me to my room, grounds me, and tells me I can only come out to go to school. It's the worst day of my life. I can hear Dad yelling at Hanna over the phone, "You're a bad influence on Alice." My own dad is acting like Hitler. He wants to 'prevent the spread of Jewish influence'. Hanna's influence *and* mine. That's when I decide to write what became my famous letter to the editor of *The New York Times*.

A SAILOR OF MY OWN

If a German plane flies over the city, I bet a boy from
P.S. 84 will be one of the first to see it. The boys in my
class are always thumbing through cards that tell you how
to identify enemy planes. Of course, grown-ups, Air Raid
Wardens like my Dad, also volunteer to go on the roofs to
warn us. We have blackouts so the enemy can't find New
York City, and when Mom pulls the blackout curtains shut,
I can only make out the flashing red lights of a police car
cruising towards the park. But they say the worst danger
comes from the German submarines and I can't help
thinking about all our poor sailors.

Mom and Dad and I go to a luncheonette near the
Brooklyn Navy Yard and the streets are a sea of slim-
hipped sailors, their bellbottom pants flapping like sails. I
want one of them to wink and smile at me. I want a
romance like the movies, with a sappy beginning and a
weepy goodbye, and "I'll Be Seeing You," on the
soundtrack. But there's Mom telling me to watch the cars
at the crossing and Dad outside the luncheonette.

"Come on! Come on! Let's go girls, I'm starving." He yells. I pull up my knee socks, straighten my plaid skirt, twirl around on the green leatherette stool under hot florescent lights and order a grilled cheese sandwich. The cheese and toast melt into bliss, and I'm completely alone, just waiting for my date.

When I'm off to roll bandages at the Red Cross, three sailors get on the IRT. One looks at a New York City guidebook and another studies a map. I want to say, "May I help you?" but they aren't lost and don't ask. Actually, I'm sure they don't even see me. My head is there, but the rest hasn't caught up. Even *I* know this. It sounds silly, but I'm a girl, I'm thirteen and I'm getting sillier every day. It doesn't matter that there's a war on.

I want to be a pen pal to a sailor. I could still choose a soldier, I guess, but to be honest, the Army uniforms are kind of stiff and all buttoned up and the sailors' pants move along with them. Uniforms matter. I get a list from the Red Cross of sailors looking for pen pals. Saturday, I go over to Barbara's for lunch. Her mom just heard on the radio about healthy vegetables that don't use up too many blue ration stamps. It's disgusting what she gives us. I mean celery knobs – she got the recipe from the radio—who knew celery even *had* knobs? Afterwards, we go to Barbara's finished basement to pick sailors. You get just the sailor's name, where he comes from, and where he's stationed. They can't tell you anything else. Like the posters say, "Loose Lips Sink Ships." I don't have any trouble finding mine. He's Aaron Cohen with a P.O. Box in England. A photo would be nice, but maybe that's too much information. We'll write our first letter and just introduce ourselves like the instructions say. It could take weeks before we get an answer. I smooth out the airmail stationery, a tissue paper sheet that folds up on itself to make its own envelope. "Wanna hear what *I'm* writing?" Barbara asks. She tugs at her new white Peter Pan collar and she won't shut up. Sometimes I think the best thing about her is this finished basement. I know right away I'm going to need to be alone. I grab a chocolate cookie and tell her I'm going to finish at home.

Mom said I have to let Aaron know how old I am, so he doesn't get the wrong idea. I start writing about how we're learning algebra and I hate it, but that sounds boring *and* childish. Then I try something about the snow in the park. I do a pretty good job actually—but it might make Aaron sad to be stuck on a ship and not be able to see the seasons change. And that's when I get the idea that I won't write about my stupid thirteen-year-old life. I'll write about my cousin Hanna's life instead. I know her pretty well and I'll make up the rest.

Aaron and I are into it: three months and exchanging letters fairly often. He writes about the pubs in England, describes his hometown, Ann Arbor, Michigan, where his dad owns a department store and his kid brother is becoming a whiz at math. He says they have a basketball court on the base, but he also tells me what he's reading and since I read everything, we have a few literary exchanges. He thinks I speak four languages and teach piano. It's sort of Hanna-ish, but I leave out that she works in a glove factory because what can you say about that? I tell him I was raised in Latvia—so was Hanna—and that I came to New York right before the war to escape the Nazis like she did. That creates sympathy for my main character, which my English teacher says matters. Aaron wants a photo. The next time I see Hanna I tell her I need a picture of her for my album. I even ask her to give me a packet of sticky black corners. I choose a photo that shows off her amazing hair. You can't tell it's red of course, but you can tell it's thick and wavy. Aaron says I'm very pretty. I love his letters and he writes back fast, so he must like mine. I want to send him a food package, maybe a salami. Instead I tell him about that poster, "Send A Salami to Your Boy in the Army." He thinks it's funny too, you know, because it's supposed to rhyme but doesn't.

And then suddenly Aaron's ship is in the Navy Yard, our own Brooklyn Navy Yard. He's getting a pass this weekend and can't wait to meet me. He's about to find out I'm just a stupid kid. How come I never thought of this? I keep hoping his leave will get cancelled, because even though I'm not paying too much attention to the war anymore, the *Times* is at the door every morning and the armed forces are, like they say, "fully engaged". No such luck. I call Hanna.

"I need your help." I confess and tell her the plan.

After she stops yelling at me for abusing my God-given talents—she doesn't even believe in God—she says she'll do it.

"Not for you, Alice. But for this poor sailor who shouldn't be made to feel like a fool. The guy is fighting our war and you tricked him."

I'm lucky Mom and Dad are off to Grossinger's Hotel in the Catskills again and Hanna's supposed to stay with me, so Aaron can meet her here. She promises to be the Hanna of the letters. She reads every one. I have his tied up with a rubber band and I keep copies of mine. That's what writers do.

"So, I'm a piano teacher?" Hanna says. "What's wrong with stitching gloves? Not fancy enough?"

"I think it's great you have a steady job and can support yourself. But you *are* getting some piano students. It's just I don't know anything about a glove factory. And this way I can talk about music. I know a lot about music."

I play cello in the school orchestra. I'm not very good, but when you put your nickel in the slot and lift your cello case over the turnstile, it doesn't matter how bad you play because everyone on the subway platform just thinks you're a musician. Seeming is more important than what is actually true, like my English teacher always says about Shakespeare. And like what we're doing to Aaron Cohn.

172

Aaron Cohn is cute, too short to be handsome, but wiry, with a blond crew cut. His sailor pants fit tight over his butt, cling to his thighs and flare out from there. Hanna introduces me as her kid cousin. At least that's true. But after Aaron shakes my hand, like the song says, 'he only has eyes for' Hanna. She plays Hanna perfectly: she twinkles, she rustles, she tugs at her bolero jacket and straightens the seams on her silk stockings when they're perfectly straight already. The guy must be going crazy. Before I excuse myself to do homework, she manages to mention a book from our letters. I think she's even read it.

After they go out, I try the latest Laura Ingalls Wilder, so I don't have to think about them together. I also find a few chewing gum wrappers and remove the tinfoil I'm collecting for the war effort. The key's in the lock. Hanna's alone, but her lipstick looks smeared. Maybe it's just from eating.

"So, what did you think? Isn't he swell? Isn't he the cat's pajamas?"

"You don't need to use slang, Alice. It's unbecoming in an educated person."

"OK. OK. What do you think of my pen pal?"

173

"He's sweet. Kind of a hick. Young for his age. I guess that's why he got taken in by a young girl."

"Oh Hanna. That's mean."

"Sorry, Alice. But you really put me in an awkward position. It got tiresome playing me like you wrote me. Anyway, you won't have to worry about Aaron Cohen. He's shipping out tomorrow. And the next time he crosses the Atlantic he'll be on his way home to Michigan."

"Can't I keep writing to him?"

"Just wait longer between letters. Your game is pretty much over."

Well maybe *that* game, because after I make sure Aaron Cohn isn't dead or anything bad like that, I fall in love with Eugene Gluck at summer camp. Eugene plays the saxophone and he does "Stormy Weather" every night. It's his only song, but it drifts down to my cabin from his, just like the mountain rain. Some nights it's the only sound I hear before Taps.

In August, we find out the war is over, really over. The counselors build a bonfire at the top of the hill overlooking the Catskill ridges. Someone sends up fireworks. Red, white, and blue sparks fill the sky. The booms echo again

174

and again and hang over the valley. We all sing "God Bless America." People cry and hug each other. Eugene hugs me, but he hugs some other girls too. The air gets cold. Eugene drapes his leather bombardier's jacket over my shoulders just like the movies. He pulls me into the bushes and kisses me. It's wet and messy and it feels very unsanitary. He puts his tongue in my ear and I like that even less.

When I get home, I tell Hanna about my crush on Eugene Gluck.

"I waited all summer for something to happen."

"So...did it?"

"Yeah. Why does everyone make such a big fuss about kissing? It's supposed to feel good. But it doesn't."

"You're probably not doing it right. You have to do it right to make it feel good. Then it feels so good you never want to stop."

"I don't believe you."

"You're standing, OK? You have to face the boy and lean against him. You want to feel his whole body against yours right down to your knees. You'll like it. Trust me." She grabs me like she's going to show me.

"It's OK. I get it."

175

I can't try her technique for months. Eugene lives on Long Island and finally comes to see the Brooklyn Dodgers with his dad. He says they're having their best season and will probably win the pennant. But what can I say? Hanna's right. That whole body business really works.

SECRETS AND LIES

When the phone call comes, Dave grabs the receiver, his mind already out the door. Shirley is handing him his hat and coat—he was ready to leave for the factory—and she raises her eyebrows. Who could be calling this early in the morning? His son cries, his daughter bangs a spoon on her high chair tray, and Shirley taps her foot, waiting for him to go so she can help the children.

The heavily accented voice on the phone comes through like it's in the room with them.

"Allo. You dere? Dovid Feldman? Dovid Feldman from Varsaw?"

"This is David Feldman."

"Allo, Tata. Is your dotter, Sadie."

"Just leaving. Call you back," Dave manages to blurt out. He tears a sheet from the pad on the table, reaches for a pencil stub, and writes down the number. The woman said she was calling long distance from Toronto.

"Business," he tells his wife, her brows lifted, her face a question. "How they get this number, I have no idea." He pecks her on the cheek and leaves fast, but remembers to close the door soft without slamming. The woman said she was his daughter Sadie. Now? In 1947? Must be some stranger trying to pull a fast one.

Dave came over from Poland ten years ago to be with his older brothers and sisters on the lower East Side. They still spoke Yiddish, but they were raising American children. It was at Ellis Island he first saw Shirley, pretty, young, blue-eyed, and as blond as a shiksa. She started in on him about the trip, about her fears of war, about the mother and father she left in the Ukraine. Shirley had an aunt in Texas, but she wasn't going there. She wanted to stay in New York City. She seemed to like talking to him. He knew he wasn't a handsome man, with his round red face, his early paunch. He didn't speak, well even in Yiddish, and he often didn't know what he was supposed to say. But he made up for it by listening to everyone else and repeating what they said back to them. It wasn't hard because he was the youngest of six and a life-long listener. That's why women liked him.

His oldest sister Sarah had come to meet him at Ellis Island. Sarah also took Shirley under her wing, found her a room and a job with a furrier in the garment district. Shirley had good English she learned in the Ukraine, and she worked as a receptionist. But she was so pretty, she also did some modeling. Once you saw Shirley in a mink or a sable, you had to have that exact coat. Sarah invited her for all the holidays. And Dave started taking Shirley out for lunch. He worked only a few blocks away at a place where they made ladies underwear, so he always had a pair of stockings or a lacy slip to bring her, even with the shortages. By the spring of 1942, the news about Warsaw was so terrible. Everyone feared the worst. He and Shirley had already been together, and she expected him to ask her to marry him. And he did. Such soft skin. And the fine blond hair in her private places. So young. A virgin. He had never known anything like it. He was a lucky man. Right away, he had called Sarah.

"I need to see you," he had said to his oldest sister, the matriarch of their family. And naturally Sarah invited him over.

"So? What's going on with you, David?" Sarah asked when she handed him a glass of schnapps. "You, the brother I only see once a month at the family meetings."

"I, uh, I—Shirley and me—we're getting married. I need you…." He blurted it out. How else?

"What are you talking about? You can't get married. You are already married, David, you seem to have forgot. Your wife and child…they are in Poland. This is not a legal marriage. You and Shirley? I will not allow it." Sarah took her glasses off and wiped them with a handkerchief. Like she could maybe see better.

"I think Shirley is pregnant."

"Just a minute. You made this child, this Shirley, pregnant? You sure?"

"Pretty sure, Sarah."

"This I can't believe. You take this young innocent girl. She trusts you like your her older brother and you do this? What kind of a person are you, David? I don't even know you." Sarah slapped his face hard enough for tears to spring to his eyes. She was a strong woman, this judge, his sister Sarah.

"I'm a lonely person. Shirley's a lonely person," David pleaded, his hand on his cheek, still smarting from the slap. "The war. I have nothing from Minna in two years. Please, Sarah… try to… Shirley and me…we are alone."

"What are you talking about, alone? You have a family. The Feldman family is not enough for you? We bring you here, we want to bring Minna and Sadie too. But we can't. And Shirley? After I help her? This is how she repays me?" She sniffed the acrid smell from the kitchen.

"Look what you done. I burned the brisket. You got me so *fatummeled* I burn the brisket. Not even a good dinner we have now. I don't know you, David Feldman. You are a stranger."

"No, Sarah. I'm not. I'm your brother David. And I need your love. That same love you seem to have no trouble giving to strangers."

Sarah had called him only a few days later. And over Shabbos dinner, she told him she'd been thinking and thinking about his unborn child. Like Dave said, it had been over two years since Hitler went into Poland. No word from a single relative. A ghetto with barbed wire there in their city. And very clear Hitler's plan to kill the

Jews. Sarah read *The Jewish Daily Forward* religiously like it was her religion, this paper.

"It is a life. Your unborn child," Sarah told David at the table with the white lace cloth and the heavy brass candlesticks she brought from Poland. "A Jewish life. Who knows whether you will ever see them again...Your Minna, your Sadie. So...I decide I must support you, like you say. To give you my blessing, like you ask. You can marry Shirley. You will never hear a word from me about this. So, eat, David. Take some chicken. The dark meat, your favorite."

She swore her brothers and sisters to silence. And at the next Feldman Family Meeting, Sarah tapped a knife on a glass and said she had an important announcement. She told them her brother David Feldman had married Shirley Pincus. No fuss. A Justice of the Peace. They were having a little celebration tonight after the meeting. A toast to the new bride and groom. There wasn't a peep. Everyone pumped Dave's hand up and down, shook Shirley's hand too, kissed her on both pink cheeks, and didn't even glance at the slope of her tummy, this once skinny girl. What Sarah Feldman said around here was law. If David

Feldman left a wife and child in Warsaw, that was history. Until the disturbing phone call this morning, so many years later.

Dave takes the bus uptown to the factory. This woman who called. This woman said she was his daughter. Was it possible Sadie survived? He didn't think about Minna and Sadie anymore—but he had nightmares—the crematorium, the skeletal bodies bulldozed and piled like garbage. The films he saw came into his dreams. He began tossing in bed, throwing off the covers, sitting bolt upright, Shirley putting her arms around his chest.

"What is it? What's wrong?"

His child, that serious Sadie, always with her nose in a book. Crying when he left for America.

"Tata...Tata, don't go." Only nine. She would be, let's see, nineteen by now. A grown woman...Almost Shirley's age. No. It can't be. It's already 1947. Minna, his wife, must have perished in the camps. But if Sadie, by some miracle, got through, certainly they would have heard by now. The phone call must be from some strange person pretending to be his daughter. This person got his name and phone number. Wants money. Knows he's married. Living the good life in New York. That's it. Maybe even blackmail. He won't call back. He takes out his wallet. Pulls out the paper with the phone number. He starts to crumple it up, but flattens it out and slips it back.

His friend Leon calls and says they need to talk, not over the phone, about "someone related to you". Is it possible Leon knows too? That he's heard about the Toronto woman. How could that be? Today. Lunch at Ratner's. Maybe Leon can advise him what to do. Leon is an educated man. Can David be a bigamist if Minna is dead?

He meets Leon at the entrance, a short, bald man, a tweed vest over his big belly, fedora hat, starched white shirt, and tie. And always with the cigar. Leon works in a glove factory. Ratner's is crowded and their business is private, but everyone knows Leon Adelman, so the hostess gets them a table in the back. Business happens every day here in whispers over pastrami sandwiches and chicken noodle soup. Dave orders a corned beef on rye. With fries. It comes fast. He doesn't even know what he's eating.

"Hey, Dave. You see what I'm saying? This Hanna. Your relative. She's smart. She could be very effective." Leon takes a big drag on his cigar. Smelly.

"What relative? You know a relative of mine?" When everything comes down, it comes down like a ton of bricks.

"I'm talking about Hanna Gottlieb. Hello, Dave? Where is your head? The woman you sent me to work at the glove factory. The redhead."

"Of course, Hanna. She's not my blood relative. She's the Latvian niece. From Sarah's son-in-law, Abe. He brought her here before the war." Nothing to do with the woman who called from Toronto. A relief. But what if that woman is really Sadie. Such a wonderful child she was. But Leon keeps talking, trying to get his attention.

"I'm not going to beat around the bush, Dave. I want Hanna Gottlieb to run for City Council. She keeps rising in the union. She would be a councilwoman supportive of our cause. Someone who understands the needs and interests of the working man. I want you, my friend, to test the waters. You know these Tammany Hall people best. They talk to you. They're suspicious of me. Check Hanna Gottlieb out. See if she has a chance."

"They don't like you, Leon, because you're always with the big words. It makes them feel stupid. Me? I don't make anyone feel stupid."

"Whatever you say. But check her out. See if she has a shot. Hanna would be the kind of councilwoman we need right now. Especially with LaGuardia as Mayor. We have a chance to make history in New York. But you know those Irish. Our local Democrats. And they have the power. Hanna's Jewish is bad enough. That we can deal with. We got mostly Jewish voters in our district. But you gotta see if they have anything on her."

"What could they have?"

"Oh you know, stuff. She's a union leader. She's active. They're always looking for Reds these days. Lots of Jews are Reds. Can't run a Red. You gotta check it out."

"OK," Dave says. "I'll talk to my guy who knows the other guy with the agency. He can find out." He pushes away from the table. He's left half his sandwich. "Gotta get back to the floor."

"Don't forget. I need to know by June. Otherwise, it's too late to get her in the primary. I already spoke to Hanna.

She's ready to do it. The lunch is on me. Whatsamatta? The corned beef off today?"

Any other day this thing about Hanna would be big news. A Councilwoman, yet. The woman is going to go places. And Dave found her. Educated, not City College like Leon, but at school in Riga. Perfect English. He met her at a Feldman Family Meeting. Looking for work. Dave got her that first job in Leon's glove factory. If Hanna Gottlieb gets to be a councilwoman, Dave Feldman will be the kingmaker. She'll owe him. Power corrupts, like they say. But even without power, he's a corrupt man. He acts like his life started in America. And he does it day after day. And look what he did to the Feldmans. They're loyal to him and to his young wife Shirley, instead of to the truth.

Dave spends the afternoon reaching his friend who knows someone who knows someone else in the FBI. See what they got on Hanna Gottlieb. That brilliant Leon couldn't get away with this, but Dave can. No one thinks a simple man is important enough to watch. He's invisible. Except not so invisible after all. That woman found him.

187

She found David Feldman. Even an ordinary name. And she found him.

Two days later, word gets back. They have a file on this Hanna Gottlieb, his informant tells him.

"She's known to the FBI. You'll have a hard time running her, even in the primary." Dave knows how these people think. They see Communists everywhere. You can't get away from J. Edgar Hoover. The guy's nuts on Commies. Hanna's case and his own work—he's manager at the lingerie factory—keeps him too busy to do anything else. He doesn't call the Toronto number, although he's pulled out the wrinkled paper so many times it's now gray. He doesn't need it. He knows the number by heart.

But Leon won't stop even after he hears about the FBI file. "Who doesn't have a file?" he tells David. "Hanna says it's nothing much." Leon wants to put up a fight. Take Hanna and meet with the local Democrats. She's an attractive, well-spoken young woman. Twenty-seven. Just married. With a future. Maybe they can convince these guys Hanna can win a seat on the City Council.

Dave goes to the candy store where there's a private phone booth. He drops in a coin. Waits and calls. The phone rings and rings. No answer. And now he feels bad. Suppose it *was* his Sadie. And he waited too long. And she thinks he doesn't care about her and won't call back ever. Selfish. He lost his daughter, again, he lost her. He killed her, tore her out of his life and killed her. He didn't need Hitler. What kind of a person is he?

Each night Shirley gets naked, wraps her body around him, rubs her pretty toes up and down his leg. Nothing. He feels nothing.

"You OK, Dave?" She kisses him full on the lips, flicks her tongue, creeps down to his groin.

"Just tired, honey."

His son Jakey runs to meet him like always. He rumples Jakey's hair. That's it. He reads him a story and tucks him into bed. His little girl, Sylvia, named for his dead mother, hands him a cookie.

"Daddy, eat." A pretend nibble he doesn't take like he always does. He eats the whole cookie without thinking and makes Sylvia cry.

"What's wrong with you Dave?" Shirley says. She gives Sylvia another cookie. Sylvia sniffles, her black hair in her eyes. Too bad the child looks like him, not like her mother.

But, Dave isn't even there. He's in Warsaw. In the apartment in Warsaw. He hasn't thought about the place in years. Now, he sees it like yesterday. The old kitchen cabinets. Painted blue, they were. And Minna setting the table. With Sadie helping her. His real family. What was he thinking? What was the matter with him? A greenhorn. A man with horns. A bull. A beast. At first, like in the winter of 1939, when he could finally afford it, he did try to send for them. He tried hard. But it was too late.

He goes to the candy store again. No answer. It's two weeks since the phone call. Refugees stay on people's couches. They move around a lot. He's seen enough to know. This Sadie, the caller with the heavy accent, *must* be his daughter. A blackmailer wouldn't stop calling. What does she look like now? What did she do to stay alive? Was she there with Minna when they led them to the crematorium? His daughter must have suffered something terrible. While her own father is here in America living off the fat of the land. A fake husband. With two illegitimate children.

It's time for the hearing with the local Democrats. At the last minute, Leon insists Dave go with Hanna. If Leon went, he's such a smartass with his legal language – he wanted to be a lawyer, but couldn't afford law school—he might hurt her case.

"Hello, Uncle Dave," Hanna says at the door of the public school they use for meetings.

"Thank you so much for coming. You are a good man, such a help to me always." The young woman gives his hand a firm shake. She speaks beautifully, better than any of them. Abe's niece is dressed in a black suit. Bright red hair. Green blouse. She looks swell. Classy. Maybe they will like the hair, red like the Irish. But this Hanna's too classy for the Irish of Tammany Hall.

"You know, Hanna," Dave warns her. "We're a Jewish district and you could win. But these guys, they don't like Jews. They don't like Communists. They won't want to put you on the ticket."

"Well," says Hanna. "I stay away from synagogues. It's true, I supported the Russian revolution, but I don't have much to do with Communists in the United States. You know, I sign a petition. I go to a rally. Maybe send some

191

money to an organization to help workers. Like pretty much everyone we know. Nothing special. But that's it."

"That's why we're meeting with them." He's sure there's more. She isn't telling him everything. She has secrets too.

A long table. On the table a thick—too thick—folder. Donovan. Doyle. An Italian. But that DeMayo is a boy. Too young to have much of a say. He and Hanna take chairs facing the table and stare at the American flag draped over a chalkboard. In the daytime, this is a classroom.

Dave talks directly to the Irishmen. He tells them what Hanna's done for the union, for the Democrats. How respected she is. He had told Hanna to be quiet. He's heard her when she gets worked up. He lets the Democrats talk. They ask Hanna and she answers short like he told her. He can tell they don't believe a word she says. Donovan doesn't pretend. He snorts and stares at Dave.

"Ah, you Jews. Union leaders. Friends of the working class. But somehow you manage to be rolling in dough, don't you? Always got an angle. You just Jew everyone down."

Dave feels accused and so he misses a chance to defend Hanna. He lets that bastard off. Donovan, Doyle and company stand up and he and Hanna are out the door. Ten minutes in total. That's it.

"It was all right, Hanna. You looked good. You talked good. I don't know whether we convinced them, but we did our best." He was lying. Surely, he could have made a better case.

"I wanted to punch that Donovan. Did you hear him?" Hanna says, clenching her fist. "You know that's the way it starts. And then…well look what happened to me and my family, and yours. It's people like that—these so-called God-fearing people—who took everyone and everything from us." Hanna unpins her brimmed hat and shakes out her hair.

"But even they have to see I can get the votes. That's more important than how much they hate us, right?"

"Sure. You're smarter than the whole lot of them." He should have said something. Get it away from Jews in general and back to one person, Hanna Gottlieb, who could win a seat for them in the City Council. That's what he would have done only a couple of weeks ago, when he was a respectable husband and father. Not the man who abandoned his family and worse yet, hung up on a daughter who survived the camps. But maybe, like Hanna, he should be angry. What about the bastard Jew-haters who destroyed his family, who took his wife and child to the camps in the first place?

They turn Hanna down two days later. They won't let her enter the primary. She's crushed. Leon, too. The three of them go out to the local bar for a drink and make a curse with every glass. Anti-Semites! *Clink.* Bastards! *Clink.* Enemies of the people! *Clink.* They drink too much and stumble out into the night.

The next morning Dave calls the Toronto number. Seven rings. Eight. Wait. Ten. Maybe the phone is in a hallway, a dark hallway smelling of stale garlic in a rundown building. He gets to picturing his Sadie walking down the hall to the phone. A tall—his Minna was tall— young woman. Someone speaks to him.

"Yes?" the voice asks. Wait. It's a man.

"You have, maybe, a Sadie Feldman there?"

"Sadie…" the man shouts. "The telephone. For you."

A minute later.

"Allo…Dis Sadie Feldman. Who callink?" He can hear her soft breathing. Is she sick? Is she all right?

"Sadie. This is your father, David Feldman. Your father. From New York City."

"Ah, Tata. You call."

"Of course, I call," he says to his daughter, in Polish. "Why wouldn't I?"

BLOOD

The last truck pulls away from the loading dock and rumbles on towards the city. Abe checks his watch – 6:32 - only two minutes late. It's always a push to get his trucks loaded and out on time. But morning after morning, even though he can give the job to his foreman, he wants to be there to make sure everything goes smoothly. Sometimes, it's a faulty oven, other times, a driver comes in late or a truck breaks down. It's always something and if you're the boss, it's always *your* something.

The sun rises and the sky becomes a hazy blue-gray. It's going to be a hot day. Abe inhales the freshly baked bread and rolls, eases himself down to the platform, dangling his legs, staring onto the now empty lot, silent after the busy morning. Right here on the loading dock, his brother Sol sat beside him, on a hot August day like this one, in 1939. The white baker's coat Abe gave him for the visit covered the tops of his shiny brown shoes. Sol went back to Latvia two weeks before Hitler took Poland. Stubborn. He wouldn't listen. Foolish. Convinced he had

196

time. One terrible decision and that was it. Abe will never see his brother again. Gone. Finished.

He's held on to hope through all the years. Since they heard nothing, maybe Sol and his wife Lotte were alive, stranded in a Displaced Persons camp, unable to get word through to them. The agencies had no information even months after the war ended. But last week, his niece Hanna goes to a meeting of Riga survivors, asking, asking. Finally. One of the women at the meeting knew Sol Gold. She last saw him sweeping the streets of Riga with a work crew from the ghetto. His proud brother bent over a broom and dustpan like an old woman street cleaner. Sol's name is not on the lists of Latvian Jews who survived the mass shootings in the fall of 1941 or on the even fewer list of who made it through the camp at Kaiserwald. And the wife, Lotte? German officers took her from the ghetto and kept her for more than two years. Such a beauty, that Lotte. They killed her too. And Hanna's father, his brother-in-law Otto, never even got to the ghetto. Poor Otto was murdered by a Latvian sniper before the Nazis reached the city. All they needed for a killing field were the streets of Riga.

Blood again in those familiar streets. Murderers. The craziness of 1905. Abe was playing hooky from school. Fourteen. A hothead. And the men and boys, thousands, were marching along the riverbank towards the railroad bridge. Blocks of ice choked the river. He ran to join them. Felt the heat of the bodies. The shouts. Protesting the Czar, they were. Jews from the workers Bund. Factory workers. Latvian revolutionaries. Pushed forward almost off his feet. A line of soldiers guarded the bridge. Someone threw a rock. Then others. He picked up a large rock, felt its heft in the palm of his hand, aimed for the nearest soldier. Got him in the forehead. Blood streamed down the soldier's face like paint from a bucket. His target staggered, fell forward. The soldiers fired into the crowd. Abe jumped over the railing and ran away along the embankment under the line of fire.

Abe sighs and pulls himself up from the loading dock. No matter how many times he sees it, it's always fresh like yesterday. He bends to pick up an empty carton, takes a box-cutter out of his pocket, slits the seals and breaks the box down again. A stabbing pain on his index finger.

"Damn. Damn." He sucks the fingertip. Tastes like rust. He tucks the cardboard box under his arm and pushes open the door to his bakery.

The Russians killed hundreds that day in 1905. But seven Czarist soldiers died too. Abe quit school and marched with the starving workers. Mama couldn't control him. So they sent him to America. And that's the only reason he's alive. He's sure he killed that Czarist soldier with his well-aimed rock, so many years ago. He only told Solly, his good and well-behaved younger brother. Only Sol knew his secret. And the secret died with Sol.

Abe goes to his desk and the few letters left for him to sign, picks up the pen and starts his left-handed scrawl. But the words swim. Mama and Papa gone so long. His sister, Hanna's mother, dead of diabetes long before the war. And now Sol. A family. Wiped out. Only he and his niece Hanna survive. There's nothing left of Jewish Riga. All those writers, professors, doctors, factory owners, musicians, factory workers. Like they never were. He was only too happy to leave that small world where everyone knew and had something to say about everyone else. But he always planned to go back some day, see the old places, walk the streets with his American wife, Frieda, and his daughter, Alice. Never. He calls out to his secretary he's leaving early. He hears his own voice. Shaky. Rushes out to the car. The tunnel from New Jersey under the Hudson is empty, his driving automatic.

He's glad Frieda is out. The apartment is quiet, suspended twelve stories above Central Park, steaming green in the heat of the day. But he's in Riga, not in 1905 but in 1941 when blood ran in the streets again, when the Nazi bastards murdered his only brother. He pulls the blinds of the bedroom, blocks out the splendid views. Frieda has made the bed and he hangs up his jacket, loosens his tie, yanks off the bedspread and the summer blanket. He takes his handkerchief, wipes the fine dust of white flour from his brown Oxfords and unlaces them. He lies down on the cool sheets. Closes his eyes. Wakes up screaming: "No. NO."

"Daddy!" Alice shouts. "I didn't even know you were home. You're way early." His fourteen-year-old daughter opens the door to the bedroom. "You all right?" She's not always easy, his Alice, but always kind.

"I'm tired, Alice. Just very tired."

"I told my teacher about Uncle Sol and Aunt Lotte, about Uncle Otto. She asked everyone for a moment of silence. But when is the funeral?" He doesn't answer.

"I know...but we could have a memorial service, couldn't we?" Alice asks. "I remember Uncle Sol. I was only seven, but...."

"I need to sleep, honey."

Alice is used to funerals at the Feldman Family Cemetery Plot on Long Island. All Frieda's relatives are or will be buried there together, remembered there together. But his own Sol and Lotte and Otto have vanished except in memory. He's not a religious man. He left all that superstitious mumbo-jumbo behind. How can any intelligent person believe it? But to feel so terrible, to grieve without anything, any body, without a body? What he remembers about Sol, only *he* remembers. He can see them as boys together, sees Sol crashing through the thin ice of the frozen river...how he reached for him with all his strength and pulled him out, skinny Sol trembling like a drenched water bird. He knew the day would come when he would find out what happened, but he kept pushing it away. Abe tugs at the pillow under his cheek, now wet and cold. Oh Mama, please forgive me. They killed him. I couldn't… I didn't… save him. And he was your favorite.

When Frieda gets back from shopping for dinner, she takes off her shoes and climbs in next to him. She puts her hand his chest, then touches the small of his back, and mercifully says nothing. Sweet, lemon scent. He strokes Frieda's soft brown hair. Kisses an earlobe. He married her, yes, and she took his name, but she will always be a Feldman who made a place in America, who will have a resting place here too, a marked grave on Long Island.

"I'm sorry, Daddy," Alice says when he sits in the living room later and tries to read the paper. "I'm so sorry." She puts her arms around him. But over dinner, Alice sits sideways at the table and picks at her food, just waiting to leave them and go to her room. Frieda asks only whether they like her new chicken recipe with grapes, 'Veronique', she calls it.

"Vero nice" he says, trying to rouse himself, to make a joke. Frieda smiles and pats his shoulder. When she clears the table, he goes to the foyer and picks up the phone. Dials the familiar number.

"Hanna? It's all right if I come over tonight?" He asks. "Good. I'll be there in half an hour."

The streets are quiet. The Chrysler building, its crown alight, the Empire State, a shiny spire. No more black-outs. Bright again. This city, now his own, is enjoying the end of a war while he grieves, once again a Jew from Riga. At this hour, the taxi cruises easily downtown to Hanna's place. She's his only blood relative, a socialist already when she came off the boat in January 1940, so sure of herself, so sure she was right. The two years she lived with them, a battlefield every night. He would like to think she mellowed, but she didn't. Now she's on her own. An organizer with the International Ladies Garment Workers Union yet. His own niece. The child of business people. But a Gold.

Hanna throws her arms around him at the door of her apartment, a pretty studio in the West Village. Her sharp chin digs into his shoulder. She's short like he is, like all of them. His glasses fog up and he takes them off to wipe them.

"Here," Hanna says before hello even. She hands him a shot glass with whiskey. Then a tall glass of soda. A chaser. Cold to the touch.

He downs the whiskey. His hand trembles.

"You all right, Uncle Abe?" Hanna says and settles into one of those new chairs, from Denmark she tells him. No shine to the wood at all like it came straight from the tree.

He sits on her modern sofa with the stiff square arms. Nothing to sink in to. But, he has to admit, her place is nice. A grand piano with a colorful throw and the photographs he can't bear to look at. Hanna still works in the glove factory, but she's beginning to get a few piano students. And the books…so many books, stacked on shelves, lying sideways, open on tables. Like a living room from when he was a boy. He comes from a cultured family. Intellectuals. He alone a disappointment. So much trouble he had, just learning how to read. He knows he's smart, but the teachers back in Riga never thought so.

"You made the place nice," he tells Hanna. She doesn't speak, her eyes red, her pointy face puffy.

"It's hard. So final." She says, "when we didn't know…."

"We thought...." He stops.

"The last time I saw my dad, he drove me to the boat. With Sasha. I wish I told him how much I loved him, you know? I was only eighteen and all I could think of was my boyfriend. So silly and selfish."

"Ah Hanna. Don't beat yourself up. You were young. He knew, Otto knew, how much you loved him, believe me...All those years just the two of you. He was so proud of you."

"You think so?"

"He told me. Not once. Many times." Actually, he hardly spoke to his brother-in-law Otto. A dreamer. And he couldn't stand that the man lived on when Abe's own sweet sister Clara, Hanna's mother, died at thirty-three. No, he had nothing to say to Otto. But he wants to make Hanna feel better. And Otto did love his only child. That's no lie.

"And Uncle Sol and Aunt Lotte. They took me in when Dad married that awful woman."

"I know. I know."

"And I wasn't even very nice. They must have hated having me."

205

"Stop it, Hanna. You were a teenager. You ever meet a nice teenager?"

"I'm sorry, Uncle Abe. Here I go again. So?"

"I still can't take it in. My brother was the good one. I was bad, Hanna. I did everything I could to make Mama and Papa angry. And he's the one gone."

"Tell me about Uncle Sol. What was he like? I mean when you were boys."

"He tagged along. I took him with me everywhere. Skating on the Daugava. Fooling around with the horses at the stable. He was a timid kid. Didn't like getting dirty. He was the best student in the class, smart like your mother. But he looked up to me. He did what I did. So why didn't he listen in '39? I couldn't get him to send for Lotte and stay here. I never asked you what he said when he came back to Riga. You were there, Hanna. What did Sol say?" Maybe Hanna can help him with this.

"Uncle Sol didn't fall in love with America, that's for sure. He thought New York was noisy and dirty and the people were common and rude. The more he talked against it, he more I knew I'd love New York."

"Like me. It suits me this city," Abe says. "I loved it the minute I got here. The energy. So many different kinds. No fuss. No formality."

"Yeah. Me too. I finally felt free of all those stupid rules about how to act and who to be with. But Uncle Sol. He wasn't like us. Of course, he knew he'd have to leave Riga eventually. He worried Hitler would break the pact with Stalin. What he kept calling 'a pact with the Devil.' But he didn't think it would be so soon."

"You're right," Abe days. "Sol wasn't like us." He hates Hanna's left-wing politics, but it's true, neither he nor his niece wants to be told what to do or how to live. He played hooky from school and joined a revolution in the streets. And Hanna went off with a working class kid, that Sasha.

"I know we argue, Hanna, but now, we have to…" He grabs her hand in his. Her palms are cold and he rubs them. His sister Clara's hands were always cold and just like Hanna's, small and white with the palest freckles.

"I think I need another schnapps," he says.

This time she pours one for herself too. He tips his glass to hers, hears the satisfying *ping* as their rims touch.

A CELLO IN HARLEM

I dump my books on the hall table and trip over the cord of the vacuum cleaner. Mom and Ursula are at it again, having private conversations about the right way to do everything. They heap the draperies on the living room sofa, turn the rug over and toss pillows all over the place. Even the Venetian blind goes down for dusting.

"You think I should send these out to the cleaners?" Mom is holding out the beige living room drapes.

"Well, they are looking pretty drab," Ursula says.

"Time for new ones?"

"Just a good cleaning should do it, Mrs. Gold."

"So tell me, what's Violet up to these days?" Mom asks. Ursula carries the drapes into the front hall and the two of them go into Mom and Dad's bedroom.

Ursula is our housekeeper and she's a Negro, but we never talk about what that's like. This is 1948. And that's the deal in 1948. Ursula is elegant, tall and thin with an angular face and hazel eyes. Where does she live? I have no idea. Except for this week of spring cleaning and another one in the fall, she comes in once a week and vanishes at five o'clock. Why don't I ask where Ursula lives? Because I think she would find the question intrusive. "Impertinent," my mom calls a girl who says something intrusive. Maybe I don't really want to know. There are a few Negro kids in my school—one is the daughter of a diplomat—but I have no idea where they live either. And on the way to and from school, on the way to my cello lesson uptown, on the way to my friends' houses I hardly see anyone who is a Negro. Except for Charlotte, who works for the people across the hall. She's darker than Ursula and young. I've never heard Charlotte say anything except "good morning." All the other housekeepers in our building on Central Park West are Irish and whiter than we are.

"Uptown. In Harlem. That's where most colored people live," my mom told me once. White people often call black people "colored." It's supposed to be more polite.

During the war, Negro servicemen came to Washington Square Park where my cousin Hanna took me for a sing-along. We sang folk songs and union songs together. Everyone got friendly like we were all the same, no matter where we came from or what we looked like.

Hanna had to remind me that we are not all the same. She belongs to what my dad calls Communist-front organizations. My dad brought her over from Europe before the Nazis killed millions of Jews. Hanna moved into my bedroom for two years and even though it was hard sharing a bedroom with her—she's ten years older than me—I have to admit I learned a lot.

Hanna is critical of the United States and my dad doesn't like that because he's a Jewish immigrant himself and he thinks the United States is the best country on earth. But he and my mom say all people should be treated equally and fairly and if they really believe that they should listen to Hanna. She says none of the black troops who served our country and fought for our freedoms, are sharing in the freedoms they risked their lives for. We studied the Civil War in school, and sure we talked some about slavery but we mostly talked about the battles between Ulysses S. Grant and Robert E. Lee, two white generals. Hanna says black people are invisible to white people, and even though I'm a sixteen-year-old girl and I don't know very much, I can't argue with that.

Living in New York City in the modern, post-war age is not going to help you with this. The problem is if you don't know any Negroes, I mean really know them, you don't know anything. Hanna says we're all racist. I had never even heard the word before Hanna used it, but I think she's right. Every Passover we talk about how we Jews escaped slavery thousands of years ago, but we're still doing terrible things to Negroes at this very moment. My mom has a friend who employs a black person—"colored" is what she calls her too—and she refers to her as "my girl." That sounds wrong to me. This person is a grown woman. I sometimes wish I could discuss all of this with Ursula, but I don't think she wants to go into it. She and my mom get along well—something about mutual respect, my mom says, and I don't want to do anything—well, to be honest I'm really uncomfortable doing anything that would make any trouble.

I'm on the subway going uptown to my cello lesson on Convent Avenue near Morningside Park. My teacher, David Fields, is young and very handsome, not like the cello teacher at school, Mr. Peterson, who's old and cranky.

I don't practice much and I spend a lot of time choosing what to wear to my cello lesson. Last week I put on a red flannel Lanz dress, small-waisted and flared, with tiny flowers, very Swiss Alps. This week the weather got hot, so I picked a striped cotton dress but also with a tight waist and a long, full skirt down to my new patent leather Capezio ballet slippers. It's what the fashion magazines are calling "The New Look." Underneath my dress, I'm wearing a waist-cincher, a six-inch corset that pushes my waist line in a couple of inches and makes my hips balloon out even more than they already do. The waist-cincher gives me indigestion, but it's worth it to have a small waist and look pretty. That's what boys like.

I hoist my cello over the turnstile. Even if you're not very good, when you carry an instrument, everyone thinks you are a musician. I play in the high school orchestra but I'm in the last desk—the twelfth cellist practically falling into the wings when we're on stage—and I mostly try not to draw the bow across the strings when our section is supposed to be quiet. Like my best friend Ruth says, "it's easy to meet low expectations."

I may not be much of a cellist, but I am pretty musical. I have a habit of singing to myself wherever I am. On the subway, I hum aloud because no one can hear me over the clank and grind of the train. I go through popular songs, themes from symphonies and concertos and generally the last piece of music I've heard. Like I can't get the Cezar Franck Sonata for violin and piano out of my head until Gershwin's Rhapsody in Blue comes along instead. I'm sitting on the subway heading uptown, not paying much attention to anything around me as usual. For some reason, I'm humming "Old Man River" and thinking Paul Robeson. I'm singing, "Nobody Knows The Trouble I Seen..." and then "He's Got The Whole World In His Hands" and thinking Marian Anderson, about when she sang to the crowds at the Lincoln Memorial. I was just a kid, but my mom took me down to DC. Now I'm humming one Negro spiritual after another. And why? Because the doors of the subway slide open and I don't recognize the stop. Then I look at the other passengers. Everyone is black. Every single person on the train. Except me of course. I've taken the wrong train—the one that goes to Harlem.

Damn! Now what do I do? I know the station where I went wrong. 116th Street. But we are way past 125th Street, the great divide between white people and black people in our city. The doors close. I'm not sure but I think everyone in the car, three men and two younger guys, a mother with a kid and one of those folding strollers, and two teen-aged girls, are staring at me. What is this person doing on our subway, they must be thinking—or not. In a minute, we're at the next stop and I dash for the door. The cello bangs against my leg. One of the guys leans against the door to keep it open. "Thank you," I say. "No problem, Miss." He's a lot more polite to me than the guys in my high school.

I keep my eyes straight ahead. Don't make eye contact, Mom always says, otherwise strangers come up to you. The subway platform stinks of urine, just like the platform at our stop. I hold my breath. Somebody bumps against me when I get to the staircase. Maybe on purpose. Maybe not. I clutch my cello and haul it up the steps. Step, bump. Step, bump. It's slow going.

"Hey, Girlie...Ofay girlie!" someone calls out. I act like I'm deaf. Also, dumb. Is it racist not to answer? Where's the downtown train? I have to get back downtown. Only white person, only white person, only white person, keeps drumming in my head. I'm going to miss my cello lesson. I have to find a phone booth and call Mr. Fields. That's what I'm doing. I'm finding a phone booth first thing. Then, I'm going to take the next train downtown.

The street at the top of the stairs is filled with people sitting on stoops, playing cards, just standing around, leaning against buildings. It's hot. Like all of a sudden, it's the dead of summer instead of early spring. No trees on the curbs like we have where I live. I'm sweaty. I feel so white. Scared white. Maybe everyone will be too busy to notice me. Don't notice me. Please don't notice me. Oh. A few are staring. One guy on a stool doesn't have a shirt on and his chest is black and shiny from sweat. He's shouting something right at me but he stops just as quick to put his hand to his mouth and whisper something to the guy sitting next to him. Maybe they can tell I only have five dollars in my purse. I finger the nickel in my pocket for the phone. But I don't see a booth. Maybe it's on the next corner. I could be trapped by a robber in a phone booth. These people wouldn't care if I were trapped, right? They probably think we deserve it. Because of slavery. I don't see a single policeman anywhere. Every one of them must be in my neighborhood making all of us down there feel really safe.

Car doors are open and car radios blasting. Music booms out of a window. The spray from an open hydrant catches my legs and drips down to my bobby socks. Not on the cello! Kids are splashing each other and not paying any attention to me. I keep my eyes straight ahead. Headed for the corner. This is how Ursula feels when she comes to us. Only black person, only black person, only black person. I gotta stop this. It's just people up here, people living their lives in another neighborhood. Where I live practically everyone is Jewish and I don't think that's strange. You are just being prejudiced. That's what Hanna would say. I'm also looking for the downtown train. It should be on the other side of the street, but it's not. Instead there's a cloudy storefront and a long white sign with a black watch. A pawn shop. We don't have pawn shops in my neighborhood.

"Hey girl!" A loud voice up too close, way too close. Pay attention, Alice.

"This here a cello, right?" he shouts in my ear. "How 'bout you play something for me?" A tall skinny guy around my age is in my face. Damn! He puts a hand on the case like he's going to grab it. "Hey," he calls out. "Look what we got ourselves." A blast of onion and garlic. Two other guys come up out of nowhere and start toward me.

"Don't..." I manage. The first guy keeps his hand on my cello. His friends are blocking my way. They look older. Way older. "Please...don't." I manage again.

I don't know what to do. The three of them are glaring at me like for hours. The guy right in front of me hooks his fingers in his belt. He's wearing US army pants. But the other guy has his hand in his jeans pocket. He has a long red scar on his cheek. Does he have a knife or something? Oh God. This has become the worst day of my life.

"You stop that this instant, Tyrone!" someone calls out. "You all...leave that child alone! Hear me? Leave her alone."

The first guy lifts his big hand off my cello.

"Just messing with her head, old lady!" he shouts. Then he looks at me hard. "Guess we scared you, pretty good, didn't we?" He breaks into a big grin. He wants me to

217

know he liked scaring me. Then they start laughing, punching each other and laughing. They saunter on down the block together towards the corner real slow like it's nothing to them whether they take my cello or not.

"Young lady!" I hear that same voice. There she is high up on a brownstone stoop. Short skirt. Heavy legs. "Yes, you! You OK?"

"Guess so…Thank you," I squeak up at her. But I'm not OK. I'm not OK at all. The woman is a blur. I must be crying. My purse slips to the sidewalk and I bend to pick it up. "I was just looking for a phone booth," I manage to say.

"You won't find a booth around here that isn't broke," the woman is telling me.

"I gotta call. I'm missing my lesson."

"Got on the wrong train?"

"Uh huh."

"Happens. You play that thing?"

"Sort of." And that's the truth.

"Come on up, why don't you. You can use my phone." She snaps her paper Japanese fan shut and drops it into her shopping bag. She's crocheting something white and lacy like my grandma makes, and she folds that up too. She gets up on those big legs like it's easy, and she holds out her hand.

"Charlene Wilson."

"I'm Alice Gold. Pleased to meet you. And thank you. Thank you so much." I should have introduced myself right away. Would I have introduced myself right away if this lady was white?

I follow her to the first floor. It seems OK. Mrs. Wilson unlocks three locks and we go into a small, grayish room, clean, smells like Lysol and, wait a minute, lilacs. A big bunch fills a glass vase on a table near the sofa. She points me to the phone on the wall in the kitchen. I lay my cello on the linoleum right next to a wooden trap with a metal spring, big enough to catch a rat. I put my finger in the phone and dial Mr. Fields. He sounds worried. My cello lesson is one place I get to on time. He's got someone after me, so that's it. I have to wait until next week.

"My mom will pay for the lesson," I say. I'm not happy with this lady hearing me tell my cello teacher that even though I screwed up, my mom will bail me out. I'm sure that wouldn't happen here. If I were Mrs. Wilson's daughter, I bet I'd have to work to pay for a missed lesson.

219

"You sure got yourself to the wrong place, didn't you, Alice Gold. Good thing I saw you just now." Mrs. Wilson says. "Bet you could use some iced tea. Could do with some myself. Made it early this morning. Knew it was going to be a hot day, steam already coming off the sidewalk. I'm ready to leave for work, got my keys in my hand, and my lady calls and cancels on me. She does that. Always last minute. Not gonna pay me for the day either."

"Thank you," I say. "Iced tea sounds swell." Mrs. Wilson opens the fridge in her neat little kitchen, takes out a pitcher and pours us each a glass. She straightens a pile of newspapers on the counter and picks up a book that fell to the floor. She turns on an electric fan and points me towards the sofa. It's dark green and a scratchy material, but there's a crocheted white doily on each armrest like at my grandma's. On the table next to the glass vase of lilacs is a framed photograph of a pretty girl in a long white communion dress. On a hanger hooked over the door to the next room hangs a black uniform with one of those frilly white organdy aprons I always thought looked silly on a grown woman. Now that I made the call to Mr. Fields, I want to go. Still, Mrs. Wilson did let me use her phone.

She's giving me some tea. It would be rude to just get up and leave, right? Maybe I could actually have a real conversation with this black lady.

"I love lilacs," I say. The smell is pretty overpowering when you're sitting right next to them.

"Friend a mine has bushes all over her yard. Gave us ladies bunches at church Sunday. They're really early this year. It's been so hot." Mrs. Wilson sinks down opposite me in a large, green recliner chair, puts her feet up and sighs. The fan is whirring and the cool air feels good.

"Bet you never been up here before, right? Well you sure got yourself in the thick of it, didn't you? Welcome to Harlem, Alice Gold." Mrs. Wilson lifts her glass to me, but her tone is not so nice. She takes a sip of her tea. Then she just sits there like I'm invisible. I want her to like me. Maybe I can make her like me, even if I am white and stupid. I can't seem to leave and I don't know what to say. So I take a long gulp of my tea. It tastes really funny. Must be saccharin. Mom says it's bad for you. But Mrs. Wilson is kind of overweight and a lot of black people do get diabetes. The window is wide open to the street and I hear a man shouting "Give it a break, will you, babe?" A long

pause and then "Will. You. Give. It. A. Break."
Somewhere, a kid is screaming. A tenor saxophone out-
wails the kid. It's "The Man I Love" and the guy can really
swing. It's quiet as a tomb in our beautiful apartment on
Central Park West even with the windows open to the
street and the park. We don't know the family across the
hall except to nod at them in the elevator. It was different
in Brooklyn where we used to live when I was a kid. But on
Central Park West, it's not OK to hang out with your
neighbors. The people down there would say "don't
fraternize." Kind of low class, you know? These days mom
and dad and me live in fancy isolation.

A fly circles a wet spot on the little book table next to
the recliner, and Mrs. Wilson smacks him with a plastic
flyswatter. Alive one second, then one wop and dead the
next. War's over but not for flies. There's sticky brown
flypaper curling down from the middle of the ceiling with
its line-up of dead flies. And I'm stuck here like one of
them. But that saxophone starts in again and I want to
listen. Maybe it will be "Lush Life" or even better, "I've
Got A Crush On You" like this street musician can read
my mind and all the songs in it.

"Most of us are just plain folks around here, but you right to be a little nervous, Alice Gold," Mrs. Wilson breaks in. She's finished her tea. "Even I don't go to the corner where you was headed. Lots of guys there hanging out, got nothing to do but make trouble. Truth is there's no jobs for them boys once they got outta the service. Not a damn job. But you wouldn't know anything about that."

"My friend Ernie is going to school on the G.I. bill," I say. "No way would he get to Princeton without the government paying his tuition. Not too many Jews at Princeton." Can you believe I'm doing that "we oppressed people understand each other" thing? Well, believe it.

"You people always talk about that GI bill. The G.I. bill this. The G.I. bill that. I'm sick of it. I'm going to tell you, it's not for black folks. The GI bill sends vets to school. It's white vets. Most of our guys don't get to go."

"I didn't know." You want a real conversation with a black lady, Alice. You got one.

"Of course, you didn't know. No G.I. bill money for fancy educations for black men getting shot at in the war. Needed you then. Forget you now. Back to business as usual."

223

Mrs. Wilson gets up from the recliner and brings her glass to the kitchen. She goes over to the window and ties back the filmy curtains that have begun drifting towards the street on the first breeze of the afternoon. She wants to get on with her usual day. She doesn't need this lost white girl in her life, this *voyeur*. Can't believe I learned the word just last week and I already got to be one.

"I guess I should be leaving," I say.

"Yeah," she says. Then she mutters, "Shouldn't overstay your welcome." At least I think that's what she said.

"So you Jewish?" she asks suddenly, kind of sharp. "My lady downtown is Jewish. Kosher too. She's not a bad person, I guess. Just tight with money."

"We're not," I say. "I mean we're Jewish. Not Kosher and not tight with money."

I put the glass on the linoleum kitchen counter next to hers and start for my cello. I thank her and ask her if she could please show me the entrance to the downtown subway.

"No problem. I gotta go that way myself. I'm at the after-school program most days. I help the kids until their moms get back from work."

I'm not going to tell my mom what happened in Harlem. Of course, when I get home, that's the first thing I do. I tell her everything. If I don't, she generally gets it out of me anyway.

"You took the train to Harlem?" Mom says. "You were there alone? I can't believe it. You know you are really beginning to worry me, Alice. Especially now we let you go everywhere by yourself. I keep telling you, you have to start paying attention. Most people are all right, but you never know. Don't ignore me. I'm serious."

I'm getting ready for the full lecture—tuning out the full lecture, that is.

"Maybe Dad and I protected you too much. You didn't learn how to take care of yourself. It was good you found that woman, though, what was her name again?"

"Mrs. Wilson. Charlene Wilson. And she found me actually. She yelled at those guys who were bothering me. And they listened to her. Stopped right away. She was watching the street. Like Bubbe in Brooklyn. Mrs. Wilson could be Bubbe's next-door neighbor if they rented places to people like her in white neighborhoods."

"You're probably right."

Me and my cousin Elaine call our grandmother "Our Eyes On The Street," like she's some radio program you tune into every afternoon.

"Mom, what do you know about Ursula's life? The two of you seem to talk all the time, but what do you talk about?"

"Well, we talk a lot about our children. Ursula is always interested in what you're up to. Your music. Your writing."

"She is?"

"Ursula has two children herself. She's very concerned about their future. Violet is almost your age. And her son, Robert is nineteen."

"Mom, did you know there are no jobs for black men? Mrs. Wilson told me. And most of them didn't benefit from the G.I. bill after they got discharged. Didn't go to college on the bill."

"I'm not surprised," Mom sighs. "At least Robert is able to go to Howard University. He's a sophomore and wants to be a doctor. Violet is only a freshman in high school, but she's an excellent student too."

"How come no one tells me anything?"

"You're busy with your own life these days. I'm not criticizing, but you are pretty self-absorbed. That's why you wound up in Harlem."

But she doesn't start in on me again. She gets real quiet.

"You know the other day Ursula and I were cleaning out the linen closet," Mom says, "and Ursula asked me if I ever read Zora Neale Hurston's *Their Eyes Were Watching God.* We had never talked about books before so I felt flattered, like she was sharing something private. I never heard of Hurston. White people, even well-educated white people, don't know Hurston's work at all. She's a black woman and an incredible writer. There are a lot of excellent Negro writers we never hear about."

"I bet Mrs. Wilson knows them. She had lots of newspapers, but she had books too."

Mom goes to the bookcase, pulls out this book and flips through the pages. She starts to read slowly and carefully like she does. It's great. She hands me the book and I head down the hall to my room with *Their Eyes Were Watching God*. I can't wait to read it. I wonder whether Hanna knows about Zora Neale Hurston and the other Negro writers. I hope she doesn't because I want to tell her. And then Mom calls out and asks me whether I shouldn't be doing my homework. She can't stop being a mother even if something else important is happening. I tell her I did all my homework in study hall. I'm certainly not planning to practice the cello. Still, I'm beginning to think my handsome teacher might like me better if I practiced instead of worrying about what to wear every week.

The next couple of hours I'm lost in the book. I come across a wonderful part where a black woman comes back from work and can shed the skin she has to wear around her boss. The woman sits on her porch and watches the road. She can finally be herself, and she studies and judges everything that passes her way. Hurston is talking about my Mrs. Wilson and all the other Mrs. Wilsons.

Dad is coming home late tonight, so Mom and I are having dinner alone. It's fish again. Flounder. Mom thinks fish is good for you. Broiled. Plain. Tasteless. And if that isn't bad enough, there are those sneak attacks by tiny bones. I douse the baked potato in lots of butter and salt to make up for this. If Mom notices, she doesn't say anything. She's starting to give up on my habits in the food department. In a couple of years, I'll be off to college and she'll have no idea what I'm eating. It won't be fish.

"I didn't mean to be so hard on you before, Alice, but I do worry about you lately," Mom breaks in. "You really have to learn to become more alert. I bet you were scared in Harlem."

"Yeah. And it felt racist to be scared. For the first time in my life, it felt really strange to be a white person. Even wrong. It must be the way Ursula feels when she's around us. The way they all feel."

"That's true, honey. You took the wrong train once, but they have to take it all the time."

The next week, Ursula is in the kitchen washing up the dishes. I bring her one more plate from the dining room and pull up a stool. She looks at me with those hazel eyes and raises her eyebrows like 'what's up?' I thank her for suggesting Zora Neale Hurston to my mom and tell her how much I enjoyed *Their Eyes Were Watching God*. She's scooping the guck out of the drain and scrubbing the sink.

She tells me she's really glad I liked the book, but she doesn't ask me why, so I don't know what else to say. Ursula washes her hands, unties her apron and hangs it on a hook on the kitchen door. She's tucking the strands of her hair back into her neat, braided bun, and getting ready to leave when I ask her straight out where she lives.

And you know what? Ursula doesn't live in Harlem. She lives in New Jersey with her daughter, Violet. In Jersey City. She has to take a ferry across the Hudson River and then the subway to get to our apartment and to her other jobs in the city. The trip takes her over an hour, she tells me, but she likes it. She says the ferry part always relaxes her. She likes watching the water and feeling the breeze from the sea. She says it's like every day she gets to take a short vacation from her life.

THE POINT OF THE COMPASS

Dad pulls out a map and spreads it on the desk—he loves maps—and he takes a compass, puts the point on New York City and makes a circle around the point.

"You must be kidding," I say. "Not even Boston?"

"Four hours. Too far. An hour and a half. You want to go away to college? Then Mom and I have to be able to drive there and back in a day."

He slips the compass back into the desk drawer. My dad never went to college, and designed his entire commercial bakery at this desk in our living room with only a compass, some drafting paper and a ruler. I can usually count on Mom, but her lips are pulled in like a drawstring purse. They're in this together, the two of them.

"Daddy's right, dear. There are plenty of fine colleges nearby. And you could apply to Barnard. 116th Street and Broadway. Only a subway ride."

"Mooom" I say. "I can't believe you agree with him."

"Are you telling me Barnard isn't a fine school? You'd be lucky to get in."

"It's not that…." How can I explain this to them? Sure, there are good colleges around here, but I want to get away from New York City and the idea that the country doesn't exist past New Jersey, unless you count Hollywood. I'll miss New York bagels, who wouldn't? But I want to find out about the West, the Midwest, even New England. In my family, that's like being Ferdinand Magellan. How can you call yourself an educated person if you think life stops on the east bank of the Hudson River?

I run out of the room and slam my door. It ends conversation like an exclamation point and usually makes me feel better, so why am I crying? I stare into the mirror and get busy watching myself cry. How the effort distorts my face and makes it red. How the tears run into the creases on either side of my mouth. The problem is I love my mom and don't like her being mad at me. Dad's all right, too. I know it's hard for them thinking about an only child far away. Some days, I can even understand that. But it's time and I'm really ready. They should cut me some slack.

I call Hanna. She's my cousin, ten years older than me and my go-to person. Hanna got married this year and moved to Queens. She used to read this newspaper, *PM* and each month in 1943 and 1944, they published a pin-up girl for the troops with not much on except a smile. Lots of girlfriends and wives wrote to the editor saying they shouldn't excite the boys. Hanna couldn't believe it. She's from Europe and my dad brought her here before the war. She thinks Americans are puritanical. Anyway, one G.I., this Bill Kaplan, wrote and said the girls improved circulation—"the paper's and ours!" Hanna loved his letter so much she wrote to him, a perfect stranger, and they started dating and now they're married. Isn't that the best "how they met" story? My cousin always goes after what she wants. That's what I love about her.

"What am I going to do, Hanna? "I ask her on the phone.

"Is this just about standing up to them, Alice? I need to know."

I stop whining.

"Well, is it?"

"OK, that's a good question, but I don't think so. I need to leave New York. I mean really leave. Not go to a

New York-ish kind of college with New York people even if it's outside the city."

"OK. Suppose you could go anywhere you wanted. Do some research. Where would you want to go?"

"Will you help me convince them?"

"I'll try. But you know your dad. He's pretty tough."

"Actually, my mom is worse. She doesn't take a stand very often, but when she does, she really does. Like how she won't let me give up the piano until I graduate from high school."

"Well she's right about that. You'd have nothing to show after practicing so many years." Hanna's a musician. My dad's family was full of them. Unfortunately, I have just enough talent to get my mom to care but not enough to ever play very well.

"Come on, Hanna. I thought you were on my side."

"Do your research, Alice. Stop feeling sorry for yourself. You're a child of privilege, don't forget that."

Hanna's pretty tough, too. It runs in the family.

But I do what she says. Send for catalogs, read them carefully until I've got a great list and send for their applications. The top ones are the University of Wisconsin,

Radcliffe in Boston. Even Chapel Hill in the South. Way beyond my dad's compass circle. I get Barnard's application, too. Just in case.

In the middle of October, like magic, my English teacher says she wants me to apply for a special scholarship for young writers.

"It pays $500 a semester at the college of your choice." I'm supposed to send three of my best short stories. She's writing a letter of recommendation and she tells me to ask my history teacher to write one too.

"Look, Alice," she says. "It's a long shot. There are lots of talented writers out there. But they offer ten scholarships, not one, so you might make it."

I stuff the application into my book bag and allow myself to hope. Hope doesn't cost a cent. Daydreaming either.

The application is endless. The college ones, too. One college has thirty questions, mostly essays. Finally, they ask, "How do you picture yourself as a woman of thirty-five?" I answer: "Still filling out this application."

I take everything into my room and write and write. I try to sound like an interesting person, but not full of myself. My friend Ruth calls it 'making a good false impression'. She's applying to Hunter College and Barnard and she's hoping for a scholarship. She might get one, too. Her father owns a jewelry store and they're refugees. That could do it. "We got ourselves this neat refugee kid from Poland," they can brag. I can't play that card, but I really am a pretty good writer. Won the English prize in middle school. Last year, I got a story in a teen magazine. I'm on the editorial board of the Lit Mag. I also make a big deal out of cello in the school orchestra, even though I'm the twelfth cellist in the last chair, practically falling into the wings whenever we're on stage. But I will be a serious student and that's more than merchandizing.

When my mom asks whether I'm working on my college applications, I assure her I am and that I've been consulting with my college counselor. But I'm not. She just wants to get everyone into *some* college so she doesn't suggest the hard ones. I actually like doing the essays. 'Who Do You Admire Most in Public Life?' Eleanor Roosevelt, of course. I love her column *My Day*. She cares about oppressed people. Really oppressed, not overprotected girls who aren't allowed to leave home. My cousin Elaine met her once at an event at Hyde Park and Mrs. Roosevelt went over to a guy who was sitting on the wet grass and handed him a blanket. "You'll catch your death of cold, young man," she said to him. I got this from Elaine, word for word. Can't you just hear Mrs. Roosevelt with her mouth full of marbles, like she talks? I'm going to use that in my essay. A caring person is caring in everyday life.

One of the boys in my class is a basketball player and he writes to the coach of a college he wants to get into. Sounds like a good idea. I write smarmy notes to an English prof at Radcliffe and another at the University of Wisconsin. I enclose a short story, the one about Hanna coming to America. I'm not a refugee, but I have a cousin who is and she lived with us for two years. How's that?

I did get into Barnard. Damn. Ruth got in too and with a scholarship. She's so happy she's running up and down the hall outside homeroom shouting, "I got in! I got in!" Everyone is staring. I hug her just to shut her up. Lisa Schwerner walks by in her stupid green gym suit and stares at us as though *we* were the clowns.

"What's the matter, Alice?" Ruth says. "We can go together. Same subway and everything. We can practically walk to Barnard."

The packet from Barnard is on my desk, fat with cheery news and information. All I have to do is sign on the dotted line and stand there at the point of Dad's compass, the very epicenter. Of course, the two of them are ecstatic. If I don't go to Barnard, they'll be mad. I really don't like people I love being mad at me. But how can I go to college in my own neighborhood? I know every street between our apartment and Barnard. Probably every person too. My English teacher says conflict is necessary in literature; in real life, not so great.

Two days later, I get the dreaded thin envelope. "We regret to inform you…" I didn't get into Radcliffe. How is this possible? I was counting on Radcliffe. Boston's outside the sacred circle, but not all that far. Not such a hard sell for Mom and Dad. In the locker room at school, I find out Mary Ann Van Greuse got in and my average is way better than hers. Hanna says I should call the Director of Admissions and find out why they didn't accept me. Maybe it's no sports. I hate sports. It's enough I walk up a steep hill from the subway to high school every morning.

After three tries, the secretary puts me through to the Director. I can't believe what this woman says right on the telephone, before God and everyone.

"I wanted to know why Radcliffe did not accept me," I say. "I have a 96 average at a very good high school and over 700 on my SATs. Could you look it up please?" I'm respectful, but firm.

"Name, please," she says in that fake British accent. I bet if you woke her up in the middle of the night, she'd talk like the rest of us.

"Alice Gold," I tell her.

"Oh yes, Ms. Gold…from New York City. I'm sorry but the quota was filled."

"The quota?"

"Yes. If we didn't have a quota, we would have a complete freshman class of bright Jewish girls like you."

What would be so bad about that, really? Can you believe it? Believe it.

So I can't go outside Dad's circle to Radcliffe because I'm Jewish and some Joyce Mursky or Ellen Silberstein got there before me. Sure, I knew about quotas, but this is first time they crashed down on me like the gate of a ghetto.

Hanna's furious. She's so mad she grabs all the anger out of me. I'm just sad I lost a way to go to a good college and leave home.

Then, I get the acceptance from the University of Wisconsin. They probably have a quota, too, but they're so big they can handle another Jew. And even better, I get the writing scholarship so I can go to the Midwest without a big check from Dad. You would think getting into the college of your choice would be the issue. But for me, of course, the only issue is convincing them.

"Out of the question," Mom says. 'You are going to Barnard. It's an excellent college. It's not as if you would be compromising."

"And Wisconsin?" My Dad snorts. He actually snorts. "It's a hotbed of radicalism. Protesting professors. Strikes. No one goes to class."

I know they want profs out there to sign loyalty oaths to prove they're not Communists. The profs refused. Good for them. I want to go to Wisconsin. It's co-ed. And a big school. I want to be anonymous and not have any one breathing down my back all the time.

"I'm not paying for Wisconsin," Dad says. "You go to Wisconsin, you're on your own. Or you could take next year off, work in my office, and earn your tuition."

"Abe!" Mom says. "You don't mean that so stop it."

That's when I tell them about the writing scholarship.

"It's $500 a semester anywhere I want to go," I say. Mom rushes to the sofa and gives me a big hug. "Oh Alice, that's wonderful! A writing scholarship... I didn't know you applied."

"I didn't say anything because it was such a long shot."

Now we can all just *kvell*—a Yiddish word that can only be understood in context—about how talented I am.

"I sent them three short stories," I say.

"Which ones?" Mom asks and I tell her.

"Good choices, obviously." She's happy not to be fighting with me.

But Dad stays on track. "Barnard will be happy to take those checks," he starts in again.

"But I'm going to the University of Wisconsin. You should see the course offerings. And Madison is beautiful."

241

I run into my room and bring out the full color brochure. I hand it to Mom and she lets it drop to the floor.

"You won't even *look* at it? "

"There's no point. You're not going."

"You want me to be miserable? I will be if you force me to live at home."

Mom swishes out of the room and says she's going to fix dinner. She's a big believer in the policy of 'delay and avoid'. That's how she wears you down.

We don't talk over the meal. It's just slurp and clank for twenty minutes. I help clear and go into the kitchen. Mom's bent over the sink but she's not lifting a dish. "You could live in the Barnard dorm if that would help," she says when she turns around. It's like she's pleading with me. Like I'm the mom and she's the kid. I hate this.

"I can't live in the dorms," I tell her. "The packet Barnard sent says if you live in New York City, you don't qualify for housing."

"Frieda," Dad calls out from the dining room. "I am not letting Alice go to Wisconsin. That's it. That scholarship doesn't cover all the charges."

"Well," says Mom, "maybe we should give Alice some time to think about this, Abe. Wisconsin's a big university. She'll get lost there."

"You don't understand. I want to get lost. You never leave me alone. Either of you! And I can take the scholarship money and go even if you don't want me to."

I stomp out of the room, slam my door and burst into tears, loud enough so they can hear. I know what they don't, that parents have to sign a paper giving the college permission to accept the scholarship. They will never sign for the University of Wisconsin.

A week goes by. Then two. I know Mom is telling Dad to be quiet, because every time he looks like he's going to talk to me, she gives him a look, sometimes even a swift kick under the table. The deadline is getting near. Mom comes into my room while I'm writing my Shakespeare paper—Anthony and Cleopatra. One strong woman. Manipulative, too.

Mom sits down in my armchair. And in a sad, soft voice she tells me Dad is coughing and he needs to see a doctor.

"We think it might be lung cancer," she says and wipes her eyes. "I don't want to worry you, dear, but you should be prepared."

Wow. He'll even do lung cancer to keep me here? It started pretty quickly, but maybe he really got lung cancer while I was busy with myself. I can hear him coughing all the way in my room.

Over breakfast, Dad coughs so hard he spits up blood. A spot spreads on his white handkerchief. You can't make up blood. His face is red. I'm scared. Something is really wrong with my dad.

I go to school every day like a robot. Is my father going to die? How can I leave now? I can't. I have to let everyone know in a few weeks. Kids at school keep asking me where I'm going. My English teacher is after me. She doesn't want me to lose the scholarship. Senior spring is long and boring. Wasps swoop outside the window of Physics and I listen to their changing buzz, louder and louder on the approach, quiet as they fly back to the garbage can outside, until our teacher slams the window and tells us to pay attention. We are. Everyone is paying attention to who's going with who to the senior prom. I'm going with Adam.

We're not a couple, but at least we like talking to each other. And neither of us is a good dancer.

Dad is still coughing and it seems to be getting worse. I'm thinking months in bed, trips to the hospital for battering but useless treatment, Mom and me sobbing at his side and trying to cheer him up and make him comfortable. And then, the drive on the Long Island Expressway behind the black hearse to the fresh open grave in the Feldman Cemetery plot. I'll have to help them. Forget college.

I rush home from school the day Dad goes for the tests. I don't even stop for ice cream. They're both in the living room looking glum, but it turns out they don't know anything yet. And when they finally find out a couple of days later that Dad doesn't have cancer, they still look pretty glum. They say it's bronchitis and that could turn into pneumonia.

"But they can treat that, right?" I ask them.

"I hope so," Mom says, "he's still coughing."

And as if to prove it, Dad has a coughing fit and can't stop. He's sitting in the armchair near the piano, his head pitches forward, his face turns dark like a spreading birthmark. And it's my fault. No one has to say it. My wanting to leave home made my father very sick. I decide I'm not going to do or say anything to upset them. For a week I lay low, you know, go to school, come home, do my homework, talk to my friends on the phone and go to sleep. It seems to be working. Dad is better. Friday, I don't go home after school. I take the subway out to Queens. One hour, but worth it.

Hanna and Bill live in a garden apartment. That means it overlooks a common area with an electric green lawn and pink azalea bushes. The trees burst with sweet-smelling white blossoms and we sit on the cute balcony, really just a ledge with a railing, and breathe everything in. Hanna pours us a couple of glasses of white wine to toast me and my scholarship. But the brie starts melting to the edge of the plate. The crackers soften in the heat and all the energy seeps out of me. Hanna is saying if I try not to nag, Mom and Dad will come around.

"They don't want you to be unhappy," she says. "They really love you."

"How can I care about them so much and want to leave them?"

"It's called ambivalence. A sure sign you're growing up."

"But the deadline is Wednesday. I'm going to lose my place at Wisconsin and even at Barnard if Mom and Dad keep stonewalling like this."

"Don't you think they know the deadline? They're proud of you. You're the first in the family to go to college, don't forget that. It means a lot to them, no matter where you go."

"Thanks, Hanna." I throw my arms around her. She's small. I'm big and I almost knock her off her chair. "Hey, I love your place. Say hello to Bill for me." Bill's an official in the Teacher's Union and away at a conference. I check my watch and race for the subway so I can make it home before it gets too late. I don't want to worry them.

When I get back, their door is closed. I check the kitchen. Mom left me a plate of cold cuts on the counter. I take it to my room, not generally allowed in my house, and wolf it down, coleslaw, pickle and all. Then I brush my teeth, put on my pajamas and get into bed. I pick up this great new novel *Father of the Bride* and start reading where I left off. It *is* Friday after all. A gentle mom-like knock.

Mom eases open the door and sits down on the edge of my bed. She's wearing her nightgown and robe like she's ready for sleep but was just waiting up for me. She smells sweet and lemony, like she always does.

"Thanks for leaving dinner, Mom."

"You came in pretty late. I thought you'd be hungry. But honey, I want to tell you something. Dad and I have talked about it a lot. If this means so much to you, you can go to Wisconsin."

"Really? It's OK?"

"Well, just for one semester. An experiment. You'll see. You're going to miss New York. You don't realize it, but you're really an urban person."

"That's not so," I say. I start babbling because I'm giddy. "I love Central Park. Trees. Flowers. Nature. It's all out there. I need more chlorophyll. We all do. It's a proven fact." I'm going. I'm going! One semester? No problem. That's just the opening wedge.

When we get the plane tickets to Madison, they both insist on coming with me. And when I move into the dorm at Wisconsin, a brick building overlooking the lake. Dad takes out the old camera and starts shooting a home movie of me carrying my suitcase up the steps like I'm the only person in the world who ever went to college. I look around. Thank goodness, no one seems to be watching. When the taxi picks them up to take them to the airport, I study my mom and my dad. I really look at them. She's wearing her black suit, a blue silk blouse, and a soft beret. She keeps dabbing at her eyes with her flowered handkerchief. He's got on a gray suit and his best yellow tie. The tie's too wide. Old-fashioned. And they are both so small. When did they get so small? The cab driver lifts their suitcase and Mom's round hatbox into the trunk of the car. When he pulls away, they're waving through the open window and Mom's brown hair is flying into her eyes.

The clouds gather over the lake and a chill spreads through the air, but my roommate is a big blonde from San Diego and knows how to surf, and the girl down the hall comes from Brooklyn of all places, and from my old neighborhood in Flatbush. She's Catholic and went to parochial school, but she always bought her shoes at Indian Walk just like I did. The first night the three of us go downtown, find a deli and there's, would you believe, a

"New York Reuben" sandwich on the menu. When I chow down on that tender Midwestern corned beef, German kraut, and melted Wisconsin cheddar, I think I can do this. Even the girl from San Diego decides to try the sandwich, although I explain that it's not *really* a New York Reuben. The rye bread is too soft and it doesn't have any caraway seeds.

About Marilyn Ogus Katz

Marilyn Ogus Katz was an author based in New York City. Her stories have been published in numerous journals, including the Tupolo Quarterly and Hadassah Magazine. Her short story, Life List, was a winner of Writer's Digest best short shorts competition in 2015. A new collection of stories, A Few Small Stones, is due out in 2018 (Unsolicited Press). It follows one of the characters in A Few Small Stones back to Eastern Europe in 1939-1940 where he and his family are caught between Hitler and Stalin. Katz served as the Dean of Studies and Student Life at Sarah Lawrence College for almost twenty years, and continued on as consultant to the president.

More Books from Unsolicited Press

Dick Cheney Shot Me in the Face by Timothy O'Leary

Lemniscate by Chris Viner

Thoughtwall Café by Cameron Miller

An Atlas of the Interior by Jeff Streeby

Bad Rabbi by Steve Levine

Sometimes, in These Places by Rebecca Watkins

DATE DUE

Made in the USA
Middletown, DE
30 January 2020

83911752R00156